MISS REMINGTON'S STEELY (CHRISTMAS) RESOLVE

UNSUITABLE SUITORS
BOOK TWO

EBONY OATEN

ebook ISBN: 978-1-923735-04-0

Print ISBN: 978-1-922486-28-8

PO Box 2160

Rangeview 3132

Victoria, Australia

The Welsh names for Marquess and Marchioness are spelled Ardalydd and Ardalyddes in Welsh but I have written them phonetically as Ardalith and Ardalithes for the reader's convenience.

1

LONDON, DECEMBER 1815

The young lady, Miss Waverley, fidgeted silently with her reticule as her mama, Mrs Waverley, of the Pembroke Square Waverleys, extolled her daughter's numerous virtues. "She sings charmingly, but only for private gatherings of friends and family, never in public. She eschews late evenings. She reads only the most appropriate materials, and never squints at the page. Needlework is where she truly excels. She will make a fine wife for a Viscount or Earl. I trust if we take a membership, the necessary introductions will take place at the next assembly?"

The widow, Mrs Lamb, poured the tea as she listened. From time to time she nodded, but said nothing in the negative. She also said nothing in the affirmative either, leaving Mrs Waverley to rush into the gap in conversation and keep talking about her wonderful, flawless daughter, as if the young woman was not at this moment sitting in the very same room.

Amelia Remington sat quietly near her aunt, Mrs Lamb. Needlework in hand, Amelia was there to be seen but not heard.

It was an excellent circumstance, as it meant Amelia could eavesdrop with utter impunity. The discussion would never turn to her, and she would not be asked her opinion.

Not whilst the Waverley women were in attendance at least. Later, she and her aunt would speak, and Amelia would get out her book, flicking through the pages for the most suitable match for such an exemplary and quiet creature.

Did the young girl speak at all?

Amelia stitched a thread, then stored another morsel of information away from Mrs Waverley for future reference. Stitch and store, store and stitch.

"Naturally," Aunt Lamb said her first words in what might have been ten minutes. "It is a most convivial setting for match making, and far superior to any other. Our system has produced a great many happy matches. Our butler, Simmonds, handles the bookings, so please make your donation to the cause with him."

Aunt Lamb never directly took anybody's money. That would be unseemly.

"Yes," Lady Waverley agreed. "I shall send a messenger with the funds. Do you have the vouchers to dispense, so that we may plan which events to attend?"

Amelia nearly dropped a stitch at this morsel of information. Goodness, this Mama was getting directly to the point, wanting the vouchers before she departed, without parting with any money.

Amelia wound her thread about the needle, then pushed it through the fabric to make a French knot, all the time wondering whether Miss Waverley had much of a dowry to speak of.

Because a dowry was a topic that had definitely gone unmentioned during the entire meeting.

Aunt Lamb coughed into her hand and rang the bell for a maid. The maid came with a tray and cleared away the empty teacups and pot. This meeting was over.

"I do not carry the vouchers on my person," Aunt Lamb began, "as I'm sure you'll understand, that way I cannot be accused of playing favourites with any of the young ladies searching for husbands, nor with any of the many, *many* eligible and titled gentlemen who attend my functions. It is not a woman's lot to handle money, we are blessedly free from such things."

The stitches would not take, as Amelia furiously concentrated on her hooped fabric, praying she did not burst out laughing at the intricate way the women danced around the subject of paying for services. Amelia Remington had no doubt in her mind that if Aunt Lamb gave the Waverleys the vouchers now, payment would never come.

Simmonds, their butler, had proven his worth time and again, being the perfect foil for the money-handling side of the business. He had developed an art to opening the ledger and entering someone's name whilst they were dithering about payment. Once their name was inked onto the page, they rarely backed out of the deal, lest someone else see their name crossed out in that very legible ledger.

No matter what their situation, Amelia had instructed Simmonds, if the customer didn't pay, they didn't get the vouchers. Bless the man, he'd obeyed them to the very letter. After all, it was in his best interests this endeavor maintained its success, and its discretion, and Amelia's role in the operation. Yes, requiring money ahead of services was a tad mercenary, but then, so was the marriage market.

Fifteen minutes later, the Waverleys senior and junior had departed Lamb House, Amelia and Aunt Lamb none the wiser for knowing if they'd paid or not. They could check the ledger and remaining vouchers, but they were confident Simmonds had handled it.

Aunt Lamb rang the bell for the maid, who entered before the pealing had fully ended.

"More tea for my niece, and a brandy for me."

The maid bobbed a curtsey and set to it.

"Shall I ask the terrible question that was not raised at all during the meeting with Miss Waverley?" Amelia asked.

"No need," Aunt Lamb took a seat by the window. "The girl has no dowry, of that I'm sure. Her only chance of securing a marriage is to compromise a peer of some kind. If that started happening at our assemblies, word would spread faster than typhus and we'd be in all sorts of strife."

"We'd be on the street," Amelia agreed.

"Worse than that," Aunt Lamb turned to her, "You'd have to marry!"

The women both laughed, and Amelia added a jovial, "Anything but *that!*"

The maid returned with the requested refreshments. Amelia abandoned her embroidery and accepted the tea. Aunt Lamb sipped her brandy and sighed noisily. It was only the two of them alone here, and they both giggled. Amelia moved to the escritoire and pulled open a drawer to extract several curled pages wrapped with a ribbon. She then took out the family's much-thumbed edition of Debrett's and flicked through it.

Aunt Lamb took another sip of her brandy and declared, "I'll bet you a new pretty blue ribbon for your bonnet there's no Waverley Baronetcy."

"You are correct, Aunt, there is no Baronet Waverley. I cannot even find the Pembroke branch of such a name."

"I knew it."

Amelia closed the book that was so essential to their business. "It is a shame, however, as that means we are still lopsided for the next assembly. We have four and twenty gentlemen and only twenty ladies."

Aunt Lamb smacked her lips after another sip of brandy. "You could always join in."

With a shake of her head, Amelia said, "That brandy has loosened your tongue, Aunt. Nothing in the world could make me participate in an assembly, for I shall never marry."

"You may have to, to even out the numbers."

"Not if I can help it."

"Oh, come now, you will marry eventually, will you not?"

"I will not. I will not have my husband pass on a hideous disease from the continent to hasten my death, let alone die in childbed in a desperate attempt to give him an heir."

Aunt Lamb put her brandy down on her side table and stood up, arms wide for an embrace. "My darling girl, I still grieve for your mother, as you must as well. Married men can easily die as well."

The reminder of her aunt's widowed status weighed heavily with Amelia. Aunt Lamb had not married until the age of twenty-three, and had not been married long when her husband had been called away to the Navy. When the news of his gallant death had finally reached her in London, she'd fetched an Atlas to find the Adriatic Sea to discern her husband's final resting place. No, it wasn't somewhere she could easily visit to lay flowers on his watery grave. It was several months' journey away. It may as well be on the other side of the globe. That had been four years ago, and Aunt Lamb had declared she would not wed again. Not that she stopped hoping for Amelia.

Amelia took their curled membership papers and spread them out onto the floor, playing matchmaker with the names. The key was to match people's personalities as much as their purses. And their aspirations. Also, their comparative heights as well. Thin, wispy lords could be matched with anyone, really, and their constitutions would probably improve after marriage. But slim young women who could blow away in a gust of wind would not make it to their first anniversary with a brute. In the wrong hands, matchmaking could be a bloody business, but Amelia was determined to make sure nobody suffered.

Moving the papers about, she placed them at an imaginary supper table. Where she seated people could have enormous ramifications for the rest of their lives. The responsibility weighed heavily. The door to their room opened.

What? They weren't expecting anyone else. Aunt Lamb sat up straight. Simmonds bowed and announced their new visitor.

"Mrs Lamb, Miss Remington, the Ardalith of Caernarfonshire."

"The what?" Aunt Lamb said.

The man in question took off his hat and made a generous bow. "The Ardalith of Caernarfonshire, at your service."

Imaginary harps strummed in Amelia's ears as she looked upon the most intriguing face. He looked delightfully unkempt, as one who'd come from a long journey could. On him it added a layer of vitality rather than fatigue. Sparkling brown eyes under well-cut eyebrows looked down on her. Perhaps it was the angle - she so low on the floor and he standing at full height, but his legs appeared exceedingly long. Oh goodness, she was staring! Heat rose up her neck and covered her face.

"Where's Carnation-shur?" Aunt Lamb demanded.

Oh dear, Amelia wondered if the brandy had addled Aunt's senses. He could be a new subscriber. Judging by his clothes of the latest mode, he had funds. He would be a useful advertisement for more debutantes to attend their season of soirées.

With a hint of burr in his accent, he said, "Caernarfonshire is in The Lord's own country, northern Wales. Ardalith is Welsh for Marquess."

Quickly, Amelia gathered up the papers and letters from the floor and bundled them together. She stood up and slotted them onto the nearest shelf, before she turned and extended her hand in greeting.

Aunt Lamb made introductions. "My Lord, this is my niece, Miss Amelia Remington."

"A pleasure to make your acquaintance, My Lord," she said.

He took her hand and bowed neatly over it, then kissed the air above her skin. Despite the lack of contact, heat stole over her hand and floated up her arm. Any moment now she'd swoon, like the silly debutantes who barely made a peep during Aunt Lamb's interviews.

And yet he very much was worth swooning over.

As the man in swooning-contention rose back to full height, he then nodded courteously to Aunt Lamb. "I have it on good authority that you are the society matron who may introduce me to my future bride?"

"I am," Aunt Lamb fussed a little with her skirts. Amelia smiled to herself at her aunt's momentary discomfort. Perhaps she too was overwhelmed by the striking specimen of manhood standing in their receiving room, his chestnut hair thick and windswept. "We were not expecting any further appointments this afternoon."

He looked surprised. "I sent a messenger ahead with a letter, but he must have been waylaid."

Amelia had a basket of correspondence she had not yet read through. The Ardalith's message could be amongst those. Alas, with the applications being what they were, their assemblies were already oversubscribed for gentlemen. They needed more young ladies. Unfortunately for the recently interviewed Miss Waverley, Amelia doubted her family would purchase vouchers in time.

Aunt Lamb recited her often repeated rules: "Our interviewing hours are strictly between two and four of an afternoon. Please make a booking with the butler on your way out, and we shall see you at our next available appointment."

"Ah yes, well," the Ardalith borrowed some time and ran his hand through his curls, "That's rather excellent. As it's not yet four, why don't we conduct the interview right now in a minute?"

What a strange way of speaking.

Amelia had to intervene. "Good things come to those who wait. We, I mean, Aunt Lamb, will need to read your letter first, then search through her files to ascertain your best likelihood for a match, and then conduct an interview."

"Well yes, very well," he said, "But to be honest, I'm in a rush." He gifted her with a beatific smile of neat creamy teeth. "I need to sail on the tide next week, before the weather turns really nasty, and I'll take my new bride home with me."

Aunt Lamb coughed softly into her handkerchief.

Concern filled his face, "I can pay, if that's what you're worried about. The Lamb matchmaking reputation has spread far and wide, that's why I'm here. But I cannot dilly dally in London. I have work to do before the bad weather sets in."

It was already winter. Amelia wondered how bad the weather might be in North Wales?

They called Simmonds the butler back in and asked him to get the bookings ledger. He returned a few moments later with the necessaries.

"Do we have any vacancies tomorrow?" Amelia asked.

The Marquess said, "You're an excellent assistant, your aunt must bless you on a daily basis."

"Oh yes," Aunt Lamb readily agreed. "Don't know what I'd do without her."

The butler looked upon the page, his eyes scrolling down, shaking his head left and right as he did so, giving every impression there were no vacancies in what must be a full timetable.

Aunt Lamb added, "It is a very busy time of year, as you'd understand. A great many of our gentlemen clients are keen to make a match before Christmas, but a hurried match can be a terrible thing. A woman enjoys the wooing."

The Marquess ran his hand through his hair again. Amelia's fingers itched to replace his.

He sounded as if he might apologise. "Under any other circumstances, I'd agree with you. As I'm in a rush, I'm prepared to pay extra for a willing woman."

Now it was Amelia's turn to cough, in shock and … she wasn't sure what the other thing was. A strange warmth unfurled somewhere inside.

Shock took precedence; they'd never had such a fast suitor approach them, and it quite spun her head. And as this was Aunt Lamb's business, at least on the surface, there was little Amelia could say.

Simmonds interrupted, "We have the Waverley appointment next Thursday, if they don't make it, this gentleman could take their place?"

Ah yes, the shy Miss Waverley. Even Amelia didn't think that would be fair on the poor girl to kick her off the books so soon. Especially as they had far too many men.

Aunt Lamb announced, "Good matches cannot be rushed."

Amelia simply had to say something, even though it would not normally be her place. "As you said, My Lord, Aunt Lamb's reputation has reached Wales, which means a great deal to us. But one poor match could permanently damage her reputation, and that simply would not do. Much less the shackled couple involved, who are destined to be miserable until the Lord calls them."

The man beamed with satisfaction. "Excellent point. And you'd know this, as I'm sure your aunt has you attached to a fine gentleman."

Shocked at how brazen he sounded, Amelia had to correct him. "I am not attached to any man, My Lord."

"Marvellous! Then this interview is concluded. I shall be back to collect you and your belongings in the morning."

Amelia was lost for words.

Aunt Lamb found hers. "Excuse me?"

"Miss Remington," The Marquess said, "She'll do me very well. I'll come back for her tomorrow. I'll treble the usual fee if you throw in a few servants."

* * *

What extraordinary luck to find a woman who could read! David beamed as he sauntered away from the Lamb residence and hailed a hackney to his lodgings near the docks. Miss Remington would make a most excellent wife. Mentally, he checked off her accomplishments as the cab rattled down the streets. Her golden hair gleamed with robust health. She looked well-nourished, and her pulse beat steadily as he'd held her hand. Definitely a sign of a good constitution. It was a technique he'd learned over the years checking horses and cattle. But it was the reading part that seriously impressed him. An excellent skill, and something that would be useful for helping him run his estates. Marvellous!

Although sailing around Britain was uncomfortable at times, it was a necessary evil of doing business around their sceptred isle. He preferred sailing to coach travel as he did not get seasick, and it was faster. A ship had no need to change horses along the way, and he could sleep in his cabin.

Sea voyages gave him the excuse not to read. He'd read nothing during his most recent sailing and had been free from those atrocious headaches for an entire week. Glory be!

His healthy euphoria must explain why he'd offered for Miss Remington so quickly. He was practically a giddy lad again, now that his headaches were gone.

When he reached the Inn, he paid John Coachman and headed inside for an ale. The taproom was crowded with men who looked suspiciously like sailing folk. Oh dear, they looked suspiciously like the crew of *Lady Rebecca*, which would be sailing within a few days.

"Ahh, Cennar-fon-shrrr," a man yelled.

Yes, definitely the same crew.

David greeted him with a wary smile.

The crewman nodded and said, "The boat's sprung a leak. We'll be a few weeks yet. We can unpack your boxes if you want to go home by road instead."

Bother! That meant he'd have to consult listings and read through tables of departure times and destinations. He could feel a headache coming on at the thought of it.

"An ale please, Landlord!" He said to the man behind the bar.

He would think about this tomorrow. As much as reading bothered him, reading by daylight was a far better option than reading by a flickering candle.

2

In a bind, Amelia bent the rules to allow Miss Waverley to attend their next assembly. Mrs Waverley had promised to pay the subscription as soon as her husband returned from the continent.

A tricky proposition, naturally. Should Miss Waverley remain unbetrothed, her Mama was unlikely to make the payment at all. However, should Miss Waverley make a good match, she'd then have access to her future husband's funds.

A husband whom she'd met via Lambs, who had already paid for his own vouchers to attend and find a wife. Why would he be inclined to pay twice?

The other nagging feeling Amelia had was her suspicion Miss Waverley's family had no funds at all, therefore any match they made between Miss Waverley and an eligible gentlemen or minor lord could ruin the Lamb Overture Voucher Enterprise.

Alas, the numbers were fixed, and despite their best efforts in the past week, Amelia and Aunt Lamb had not been able to secure enough ladies to balance the attendances. Which was why, on this cool evening as the candle lamps glowed warmly along the walls, Amelia herself was in attendance. She helped balance the female side of the room, but it also meant she could steer young Miss Waverley into the willing and (as far as she knew, unfussy) arms of the Ardalith of Caernarfonshire.

His recent visit had proven himself a man unconcerned with choice of wife, only that he needed one quickly.

Miss Waverley had arrived on the arm of her Mama. Her cream-coloured dress was prettily decorated with bright orange ribbons and red embroidery around the sleeves. Not a combination that Amelia would choose, but it did draw the eye.

"I am so pleased you could attend," Amelia said, giving Miss Waverley a warm embrace. The key here was to win Miss Waverley's trust and guide her towards her future husband.

Miss Waverley replied in a voice that squeaked like a door, "Thank you."

Little wonder the woman had been mute during her previous interview. No matter, Amelia was determined to make introductions the best way she knew how. Whilst Aunt Lamb looked after the chaperones and matrons, Amelia did her magic, providing a suitable environment for suitors to meet.

"There you are!" a warm voice with a Welsh lilt announced.

She could not have co-ordinated this better if they had been in a progressive dance and knew where everyone was positioned.

Miss Waverley dropped into a respectable curtsey, and he made a return bow as was expected. Amelia made introductions and Miss Waverley wordlessly put her hand into his, allowing him to kiss her glove.

Yes, this would do rather nicely. This unfussy man would

take this young woman in hand and there would be mentions of special licences within a few days.

For her part, Miss Waverley seemed rather taken with the Welsh Marquess. Excellent!

Amelia seized the opportunity to absent herself, "There will be a waltz starting in the next set, please excuse me, I need to make sure the refreshments are ready."

Her plan could not be coming together more easily. So why did Amelia feel a pang of something behind her ribs as she walked away? Given Miss Waverley's situation and station, the squeaky-voiced debutante had done very well catching the eye of a marquess.

The night was young. There would be plenty of time for these two to get to know each other better and decide whether they would truly suit. That's what this enterprise was all about.

"I just remembered," Amelia said, as she re-approached the couple who were about to walk toward the dance floor.

The two turned to her. His face displaying mild confusion. Miss Waverley's looking more worried, as if she were about to be chastised.

Amelia had to think of something. Why had she interrupted them? It could not possibly be from a pang of regret at throwing these two people together, could it?

She threw people together all the time. It was her *business*.

"I'm not sure I gave Miss Waverley a dance card," Amelia invented.

"Oh yes!" Miss Waverley squeaked. "Thank you!"

The Marquess looked to her and said, "That's a voice to carry across the valleys."

Miss Waverley giggled and said, "Thank you. I love your accent as well."

"What accent?" He said in reply.

Miss Waverley giggled again.

"I'll be right back," Amelia said, "with the dance card. Why don't you two go through anyway and I'll find you in there later?"

The Ardalith said, "Right you are then," and steered Miss Waverley away.

Amelia tried to set her mind at ease as she sought out a spare dance card. Patrons who bought vouchers were issued with them upon receipt. But as Miss Waverley had not yet paid, she had not received one.

As she made her return, dance card and short pencil in hand, the Ardalith intercepted her.

"What silly game are you playing at here? Throwing that sparrow in my way, to keep me distracted from a golden goose like yourself?"

"What?" *Had he called her … a goose?*

"You know what I mean." He corrected himself. "I'm not one for Balls and frippery. I may be in a hurry but I'll not be treated like a fool. We both know you're the one for me, and I'll brook no argument."

It was a wonder her eyebrows didn't vanish into her hairline, such was Amelia's shock. She took a steadying breath and went on the attack. Politely, of course. No raised voices. She may as well send everyone home if it came to that. "You came here to be introduced to a prospective wife, and I am fulfilling that to the letter."

"And I've already settled on you," he said in that intoxicating burr.

Drat the man!

She pushed the dance card and pencil into his hands, "Please write your name for the waltz and deliver this to Miss Waverley on your return to the dance floor. I believe I can hear the musicians readying."

"I'll dance with her, but I'll not marry her," he said, accepting the items. "What do I need to do to prove to you that you'd be a perfect Ardlithes for me?"

Gossip would spread faster through the ton than a cold north wind. Amelia prayed nobody overheard his declaration. Her heart beat faster and faster. A young woman could so easily lose her head over this determined, handsome, poised man. "I am a business woman, I do not blur the lines between business and pleasure."

"But it's your auntie's business, is it not?"

Oh drat. That!

How close she'd come to revealing all so soon after meeting this confusing, tempting specimen. "W-ell. Yes, it is Aunt Lamb's business, and as her assistant I am here to assist in any way I can. If I married, it would leave her at sixes and sevens."

There, that should cover it nicely.

As far as society knew, this was Aunt Lamb's business. It didn't matter that it had been Amelia's idea, and that she did most of the work. And the matching, which was probably the most important part. The simple fact was no society Mama would trust their daughter's future happiness and connections to an unmarried young woman to arrange. But a widow of good standing? Totally respectable.

However, if Amelia married, there'd be no way to keep her all-consuming work from her husband's knowledge. He'd want her to give it up, or hand everything over to him.

Not a chance.

She'd simply have to remain single and let Aunt Lamb take all the praise. Lamb Overture Voucher Enterprise was going far too well for Amelia to consider ending it all and getting married. No matter how tempting that man might be.

3

Amelia particularly loved the afternoon after a match-making gathering the night before.

Aunt Lamb would be swamped with happy notes from debutantes, and hopeful calling cards from gentlemen. This was when the real work began. The notes might be addressed to Mrs Lamb, but it was Miss Remington's task to read through every note and card and calculate the chances of a good match with another attendee with whom they'd made overtures.

This was the unique proposition which set their enterprise apart. Everyone who received a voucher would also then send a note to Mrs Lamb, confidentially of course. The young ladies (most likely with their Mamas watching over their shoulders) would indicate which gentlemen they would accept a call from. The gentlemen would send their cards with the names of the young ladies they would be happy to call upon. It was an excellent way to keep track of successful matches, and also provide a convenient way for these young people to save face, should nobody wish to make a call or receive one. Or should they get too many, as sometimes happened.

Amelia knew of no other enterprise offering such a scheme, although she was sure word would get around soon of Mrs Lamb's successful methods.

It was also Amelia who read through all the applications and following correspondence. She was the one who knew how to make a good match. This hard work on her part created an excellent misdirection for the society mamas who tried to sway Aunt Lamb's opinions with gifts and further invitations. While Aunt Lamb happily accepted her bounties, she could honestly say the favours did not sway her one jot. This was the honest truth, as it was Amelia performing the analysis for potential matches. This she could do without disruption, as most people paid her no mind.

Most people, but not all.

Simmonds appeared at the study door. "The Marquess of Carnations is waiting in the front room, Miss."

Amelia tried not to giggle. The Marquess's title was something of a mouthful. She struggled to remember his correct address. "I do not have an appointment with the *ar-da-liff*. Tell him I am busy."

Footsteps sounded in the hall, and the Marquess himself walked straight past the butler and stepped into Amelia's sanctuary. "I can see that!"

He held out a pink carnation flower - it must have been grown in a hot house.

Amelia stood up and walked towards him, to accept the flower but also to make sure his focus was on her face, and not the letter-strewn desk that a woman should not be working at. If he saw the letters addressed to her aunt, or the multiple calling cards from the gentlemen, it would expose her role in the enterprise.

"I appreciate the gesture, which may be *de rigueur* in Wales, but turning up unannounced at a private house is not how we behave in a civilised country, My Lord. Please make an app-"

"-Rubbish," he said, stopping Amelia short. "This is a place of business, is it not? It's a private house when you want it to be, but you conduct all your business here. You run perilously close to being in trade, if I could be so rude." That shocked Amelia into silence. He continued, "You're trying to throw me off the scent with your impossible English rules, and I won't be falling for it. I also won't have gibbering debutantes thrown in front of me. I need someone who can organise an estate, not some pretty thing who can't sneeze without her Mama's permission."

Amelia felt ready to explode, but first, she had to get him out of her office and away from those damning letters that would betray everything.

"Please wait for me in the receiving room, I shall be there presently."

"Oh, I see! You'll be down now in a minute, is it? And how long will that take?"

There had to be something lost in translation going on here. "I shall be five minutes, precisely. Does that meet your requirements?"

He slayed her with a beatific smile.

"Then I shall stay here until you're ready."

Amelia clenched her hands into impotent fists, but not too

tightly to crush the carnation stem, as the flower was rather pretty.

"No, you shall not. You shall take yourself to the receiving room while I …"

Oh dear. She'd almost said what she was going to do. Pack up the paperwork. But why would she be doing any paperwork? Why was she even in an office at all? This was a man's domain, and the sooner she removed him from this room, the better.

The Marquess delivered another devastating smile.

Amelia quickly said, "I've changed my mind, we shall both move to the receiving room." With that, she stalked out of the room. Once she reached the hall, she turned to make sure he was following directly behind her.

What?

He was not behind her! Neither was the butler.

The butler was saying something like, "You don't need to concern yourself with those."

Amelia raced back in, to find the Marquess perusing the letters and cards on her desk.

Damn and blast. He'd ruin everything!

"What's going on here?" he said, waving his hand over the many letters across the desk and turning them over. "This is not something a young woman should be involved in. Where is your aunt? A widow should be handling this, she at least knows about what's expected from marriages."

Holding the carnation like a dagger, Amelia decided the only way forward was to brazen this out. She steeled herself for an onslaught of lies. Her heart raced, her hands turned clammy. This was a necessary deception, because their enterprise was at stake.

"Aunt Lamb is indisposed. I am merely stepping in to help streamline operations while she … is … indisposed."

The Marquess narrowed his eyes. "Such fast dissembling. You're a crafty one."

"Dissembling?" Amelia repeated the word so her brain had time to catch up to her roiling emotions. "What are you doing in a private office going over private correspondence not addressed to you? If this is the high and mighty way you handle your affairs in Wales, it might be for the best that you return to your lands immediately."

Did it move him? Did it shame him in the least that he was trespassing and meddling in affairs that were not his?

Not one bit.

He laughed.

The blackguard laughed!

A deep, throaty and annoyingly attractive laugh that sent shivers through her body.

Pouring lemon juice on her emotional wounds, he began to open drawers and rifle through them. "When I first laid eyes on you," he said, looking Amelia up and down as if she were a prize he'd come to claim, "you were sitting on the floor, up to your knees in paperwork. Today I find you doing more paperwork. Your Aunt, on the other hand, has never appeared with a paper or pen in her hands."

"What does this have to do with anyth-"

"-Your darling Aunt Lamb doesn't do any of the work here, does she?"

Mouth turning to ash, Amelia clutched at mental scraps. "It's her name on the enterprise!"

"You evaded my question." He crossed his arms over his

substantial chest. "But in doing so you've answered it perfectly. You're the one doing all the toil, and she gets all the glory."

Something warm and dangerous unfurled inside Amelia, even though she was utterly furious. Plus something else. She'd been in this room with many handsome men before. All of them had ignored her, thinking she was staff, or Aunt Lamb's assistant. If they'd thought of her at all.

The Marquess of Carnations had finally noticed her.

More than that, he'd noticed what she was up to.

Drat!

Fear made her desperate. "You have to promise not to tell anyone. I shall refund your vouchers and you may return to Wales at your leisure."

He kept his arms crossed and leaned backwards onto the desk, so he parked his thighs and buttocks on the surface. "Slight hiccup with that. The boat's sprung a leak and she'll not sail. I appear to have more *leisure* than I had previously budgeted. Miss Remington."

"Well, Mister … My Lord, that is not my problem."

"Rosstrevor." He said.

"What?"

"My name is David Rosstrevor. You think if you get married, you have to give it all up. If you marry me, I'll let you keep trading. It's an excellent endeavour, why would you want to stop."

As flattered as Amelia was that David Rosstrevor thought her business was excellent, she had no intention of taking a chance that she'd lose it. Especially not so soon after it had become successful, and had the potential for even greater glories.

"I thank you again for the offer, but I absolutely must decline. Please leave the premises, this audience is completed."

She walked out and took herself to the kitchen, where she surprised the maid. "Can you get Simmonds to make sure the Marquess is gone, and then lock the door. I do not want any further visitors for the rest of the day."

The maid bobbed a curtsey. "Yes 'm."

4

L ater that afternoon, after the coast was definitely clear and there would be no more interruptions, Amelia settled at her desk again.

David Rosstrevor, Marquess of Caernarfonshire might have left the room hours ago, but his presence still dominated.

Steeling herself for what she dearly hoped would be an uninterrupted few hours of work, she set to matching ladies to gentlemen, then writing to said gentlemen that such ladies would be accepting of a call. It was what she did for the day after a gathering, and the workflow reassured and calmed her.

But oh!

Poor Miss Waverley.

Not a single gentleman had written her name on the back of their cards. Had she made such a low impression that not one man could see her potential?

Sympathy caught in Amelia's throat. The poor young woman would not likely have a successful season if this first outing were any indication. More importantly, Amelia was unlikely to see a penny from Mrs Waverley, if nobody paid interest to her daughter.

This was why Lamb's always took the money up front. Following up payments after a match was difficult enough. Squeezing money from a tight purse after no match at all? Hopeless!

Unless?

Amelia had a wicked thought. What if she arranged for the Arda-thingy-Marquess of Caernarfonshire to pay her a call? This could benefit Amelia, too, as it could remove the prying Marquess out of her affairs. The longer he stayed in London, the higher the chance he had to give away her secret. Whether deliberately or accidentally didn't matter. Every day he remained here increased her chances of being discovered as the real person running the matchmaking enterprise.

He'd seen through their masquerade so quickly, he'd worked out Aunt Lamb was merely the public face of the business in a trice. Could she trust him to keep their secret?

No chance!

If people found out an unwed, unseasoned young miss was at the helm, everything would collapse in an instant. Good grief, people might also want their subscriptions returned, and that would spell utter disaster.

She would arrange for Miss Waverley and the Marquess to visit Lamb's on the same afternoon. That way, she'd have both of them in the one room and would be able to facilitate their mutual needs. It would not be long before she had them both off her hands and off her books, and off her conscience too as they would be off somewhere in Wales and not giving away Lamb's secrets.

Grinning to herself at how clever her plan was, she began to write the invitation to the Marquess. This would all be splendid.

* * *

An hour later, she delivered her correspondence to their footman. Walking back to her office, she saw a Marquess-shaped shadow darkening the windows by the front door.

Oh drat!

The butler appeared and said softly, "Shall I tell him you are not at home?"

It was tempting to engage in subterfuge, but he would no doubt see the footman heading out with the correspondence, and that made a farce of not wanting to face up to him.

With a steady breath, she shook her head.

After all, she'd written the letters. He could come in as her correspondence went out, because the correspondence certainly needed to go out. She was late with the letters today, because of the ard-a-liff.

"May as well let him in, he'll only come back later. Best deal with him now."

"Shall I send him to the waiting room?"

Amelia nearly nodded, then changed her mind. "No. Send him to my office, I shall await him there."

There were no more unread letters on her desk, nothing to betray anyone else's confidences. All the same, it would be handy to have the family retainer standing by. "Please, wait outside the office door, on the off chance I may need assistance."

"Of course, Miss Remington."

Pressing her palms nervously against her skirts, Amelia slipped back to her office and sat behind the desk, taking a last-minute mental inventory of anything that may appear incriminating.

The butler knocked on the door and opened it.

"The Ardalith of Caernarfonshire here to see you, Miss Remington."

Amelia rose from her seat as the man walked in. She drew an involuntary breath at the sight of seeing him again. How dare he look so magnificent in his fine wool coat that emphasised the breadth of his shoulders.

As he removed his hat, she noticed his hair had improved greatly with a recent trim. Young Miss Waverley would be a very lucky bride indeed, provided she took the opportunity.

His handsomeness almost unravelled her tightly stitched promises of remaining unwed. Amelia swallowed and reminded herself that David Rosstrevor was bombastic and autocratic. He also lived such a dreadfully long way away. She'd never see her friends or Aunt Lamb again if they wed.

Something scratched her brain about how her business would not only suffer but most likely completely fail if she and the Marquess formed any kind of attachment. That didn't mean she couldn't appreciate the man for what he was, a fine specimen indeed. A man she could heartily recommend to an unwed young woman in need of a well-to-do husband.

"Ah, good, you're here," he said by way of introduction.

"Good afternoon, my lord," she replied with a curtsey, as he was due, even if he didn't personally deserve such a courtesy. "My aunt is not available at present, but I can take any concerns you may have to her."

"Now, now, you don't need all that palaver with me. I'm here to see you, of course," he said.

Amelia felt herself smiling at a teasing thought. "If you're here on business, then it would be remiss of me if I did not remind you of the English custom, during the season, that Gentlemen conduct business in the mornings, and make calls to ladies in the afternoons."

There hardly seemed any point in trying to improve his manners or his understanding of local etiquette, considering how soon he would be leaving. Speaking of which: "You made quite the impression on Miss Waverley. She would be most conducive to receiving a card from you, perhaps a call tomorrow afternoon?"

He held his hat in his hands and shifted his weight from foot to foot. "May we please stop pretending? I made a hash of things, because I was in a hurry. I've since had time to think."

It sounded as if he wanted to apologise. Amelia held her tongue, letting the silence grow so he could explain himself more fully.

"The ship is damaged and won't be ready for weeks. I find myself needing to make alternate arrangements for the return journey. I require your assistance in that matter."

Warmth filled Amelia at the thought of him staying in London for longer. Oh dear, where had that come from? Her mind snagged. He'd already told her something about a leaky boat and his extra leisure. Did he have memory problems as well as poor manners?

"Does that mean you'd like more vouchers for more dinners? There won't be many more before Christmas, but they will resume in the new year and run right through the season."

She moved to her seat, then pulled open a drawer where she pulled out a leaf of paper to make a note. What an excellent opportunity to create more business. She then tugged the bell pull and the butler appeared.

"The ledger and vouchers for the Marquess," she said.

The Marquess remained standing. "Does your aunt truly not perform any of the business functions?"

Amelia stopped short, keeping her focus on the middle distance, not daring to look at him.

"You knew exactly what to do, straight down to business yourself. You've done this too many times before," he said.

Flustered, Amelia closed the drawer. She kept her tone clipped and officious. It was the best way to keep him at bay. "Why are you here, my lord?"

"I'm here to pay you a visit. I'm courting you."

Heat flipped low in her belly at his admission. For a fleeting moment, she enjoyed the blatant declaration that he was here not just to see her, but he was here *for* her.

Not that it could ever happen.

"I am flattered, obviously. But if I have led you to believe I was amenable to courtship, I must sincerely apologise. Please understand it is no slight against your good self. Any other woman would be delighted at such attention. Such as Miss Waverley, who would appreciate your ... ah ... attentions."

He walked closer to the desk while she talked, and moved a chair to sit himself directly opposite her. "Of course, you're flattered. I'm an eligible bachelor, and a titled Lord with a generous settlement. If you need your aunt so much, bring her with you."

For a fleeting second, he made it all seem so easy.

But only for a second. "My aunt has a successful enterprise to manage. I am needed to assist her. I must remain."

He leaned in and placed both forearms on the table. "Stop pretending I didn't already expose this silly ruse. Anyway, if it means that much to you, bring Aunt Lamb as your cover and set up in Wales."

He was too close, the intensity of him, the sheer force-of-will of him.

The butler entered with the ledger and the card-shaped vouchers.

With a scratchy throat, Amelia said. "Please place them on the desk, and get the maid to bring tea."

The moment the butler left the room, she said, "It's not that simple." Amelia leaned back, putting distance between herself and this headstrong man.

"I'll not tell anyone you're the brains behind it all, if that's what you're worried about?"

For a land-dwelling human, Amelia gave an incredibly good impression of a freshwater fish, as she opened and closed her mouth to no good effect.

"Your secret is safe with me," he said, placing one finger to the side of his nose. "Although this only makes me desire you all the more. An elegant young woman, but not so young she would irritate the senses. Wise and clever. You'd make an excellent and capable wife and overseer of my vast estates."

Did he have to say 'vast' estates, as if it was some kind of prize? Which it clearly was. Double-triple drat the man. Amelia sighed. "I hope I can rely on your ... discretion ... in these matters?"

"What do I need to be discreet about? You're a fine woman, with a sharp mind and talent to go with it. If I let it be known to all and sundry that I'm courting you, surely that's to your benefit."

Amelia shook her head. He was so many steps ahead of her it hurt. "It is?"

"Yes, it will keep other gentlemen away, knowing we have an understanding."

"But we do not."

"They don't know that."

"Please, My Lord–"

"Call me David."

"I couldn't possibly. Lord Caernarfonshire, do not belabour this point. Yes, I admit I co-ordinate a matchmaking enterprise, but I do not, and will not, put myself in contention for a match. That is for others."

He folded his arms and leaned back, sizing her up. "Why is it not for you?"

He truly was being obstinate. "How could I possibly carry on the enterprise behind my future husband's back?"

"But you wouldn't be, because I've already told you I know all about what you're up to. And if it wasn't me, speaking purely hypothetically, if it was someone else, why wouldn't he join in and expand the business? It's not just people in London who need you. I can think of many larger cities where the opportunities would arise. Why not cater to those who don't or can't come to London?"

He was being obstinate again and fraying her every last nerve. The ones that weren't betraying her by sending sparks of life through her system. "A married woman, working?"

"When she's as good at it as you are? Yes!"

"I don't know how they do things in Wales, My Lord, but that is not how things are done here."

"Please, call me David. Plenty of women work beside their husbands all over Britain. It brings in more income for a start."

"That's because they must, My Lord. The rules are different in our circles. Can you imagine how insulted my husband would be, what a terrible scandal it would be, if I continued to conduct business after we were betrothed?"

He shrugged one shoulder and said, "I wouldn't be offended." Then he pinned her with his gaze and declared, "I'd let my wife conduct whatever business she could turn her clever head to, as long as she called me by my Christian name."

"Then your future wife is a very lucky woman. Speaking of whom, I believe Miss Waverley is expecting her call. It would be most impolite to ignore such an invitation."

"Oh, no, not her. She won't do at all."

Amelia started ticking off her fingers, "She is pleasant, healthy, young."

The Marquess mimicked Amelia by ticking off his own fine fingers, "Twiddle-fingered and ninny-mouthed."

Amelia spluttered, "Ninny-mouthed?"

He laughed and relaxed his body. "All she does is twist her fingers all the time and is too scared to talk. We will never get on. Not like you and I do. This conversation is enlivening. I enjoy the way you challenge me."

Amelia blew out a breath. "Perhaps I should take up finger-twisting?"

"You're much easier to look upon as well."

Oh how lovely his words, but she had to keep them at bay lest she fall for their sweetness. They were getting nowhere at all!

"There are a great many more beauties in London," Amelia declared.

"True," he leaned in again, like a cat about to swat a very tired mouse. "I bet none of them are as clever as you, though."

If only he would stop complimenting her and making her feel so accomplished. "Please stop. Why can you not accept that I will not marry?"

He unfolded his arms and spread his hands out. "Because it makes no sense. None at all. You say you'd have to give up the business if you married someone from around here, but I've already declared I'd be happy to support whatever venture you wanted. You could expand into Wales and make matches there as well as you could here."

Every time he said words like 'here' or 'year' they sounded more like 'hyor' and 'yor'. The diverting cadence of his melodic voice would destroy her resolve if she wasn't careful.

He kept on. "Is it that you want, to be better wooed? Is that it?"

How did she explain?

He didn't seem to want to wait. "I'll admit, I was abrupt when I first arrived, and I have no experience of wooing. I do have business skills, mind, and that's why it was obvious to me that it wasn't your aunt at the helm, but your good self."

His logic pinned her. She adjusted an imaginary misplaced lock of hair and smoothed her palms along her skirts. "My Lord, I find that I enjoy being a spinster. My time and my life are my own. Yes, the enterprise is something I have created, with my aunt's assistance as the acceptable face, which allows me greater freedom to build the business and make it grow into something that is bordering on lucrative, without being obscene."

He leaned back and smiled, and it sent a cold shiver through her. This was not a happy smile. It was a calculation. "How long do you think society will accept your aunt running a matchmaking business, when she can't even get a match for her lovely niece?"

* * *

It was his own fault, of course. He should have wooed her from the start, been polite, offered more compliments. If Miss Amelia Remington wanted wooing, he'd woo her. He had to find a way to show her he was serious. He wanted her to know she could still run her enterprises to her heart's content *and* be married. Preferably to him. She had the kind of fine mind that would make an excellent overseer of his estates. It very much did need overseeing. It was getting better, but only because he did most of his business in his head. His ledgers had scant entries - his own fault for giving in to the headaches.

He only need look at the unopened books and his head began to pound. But Amelia Remington had no such ailments. He'd seen the way she read, the way she wrote. Those adorable little glasses on the edge of her nose to assist in fine writing. Yes, he'd tried wearing spectacles. The headaches had persisted, so he'd stopped persisting.

He needed someone with Amelia's intellect and clear lack of headaches to keep the books, and he wagered she'd be brilliant at assessing the right kinds of crops to plant and livestock to breed. There had to be a better way to increase the yield. She'd be good at that. Matching people had to be about the same as matching crops to weather conditions.

At least, that's what he hoped. He didn't want to admit how

desperate he was to keep things going. How much pressure there was to turn the land over to the mines.

It was lucrative, but he'd only be able to sell it once. If he kept the land producing, people could eat the produce. If it became a coal mine, people couldn't eat coal.

He cursed himself. If he hadn't made such a terrible first impression, if he hadn't been so startled by her, he would have had time to do this properly.

He would simply have to hurry up and woo her the right way.

"I have an invitation to a musical event, I would very much appreciate you accompany me to that."

"A what?"

He fetched the ticket from his pocket, "It's called a musicale, and it's in Mayfair in three days."

The way her face lit up when she looked at the ticket and read the contents. He hoped he'd described it properly and had not pulled out the wrong ticket.

"Oh, my goodness!" she put her hand over her mouth, "how did you come by such a valuable invitation?"

"They're old family friends. She gave it to me when I paid her a call. Does that mean you'll come?"

"I …" She looked like she wanted to, but was holding back.

He pushed home his advantage. "It could be good for business. Bring your Aunt as chaperone, you might recruit more single ladies to the business at the same time. Your numbers were out of balance the other night."

He watched her face for signs of interest. She nodded. Excellent.

"In which case, I thank you for the invitation, My Lord."

"Please, call me David."

5

Amelia Remington woke to the sound of rain falling heavily against the window. Hardly surprising given this time of '*yor*' as David had called it. Oh hells. She was thinking about that man far too much.

The man was also far too right. How poor did it look on Aunt Lamb's matchmaking business to still have an unwed niece? Well, it didn't look too bad just at this minute, but in another season it might. In two more seasons it definitely would. After that, Aunt Lamb's reputation would drop like a wet chemise.

Amelia had to make sure that didn't happen. It added to the pressure on her, but she was sure she could do it. She simply had to make an incredible match out of her current crop of customers. The match of the season. A match that would have people talking about Lamb's in admiring tones for *yors* to come.

* * *

A trust. David mulled it over as he and Miss Remington and Mrs Lamb rode in the carriage toward the musicale.

39

He needed to find a way to show Amelia she could trust him with her secrets and …

A jolt of brilliance hit his head.

Trust!

He would get a lawyer to draw up a trust.

Mrs Lamb looked at him with suspicion. "What are you grinning about?"

"Oh, nothing," he hunted his brain for a good excuse. "I'm thinking on some ideas for rotating crops and had a sudden moment of clarity."

"Crops excite you?"

Good, she'd bought his lie. "Ordinarily no, but this is good. You see I'm experimenting with seaweed as a potential fertiliser and weed suppressant. I had the idea whilst on a recent sailing voyage where-"

Mrs Lamb waved her hand over her mouth to stifle a yawn.

Good, he'd bored the matron from her curiosity. Now he could get back to thinking about the delightful young woman sitting opposite him. Miss Amelia Remington, soon to be Rosstrevor, Ardalyffes of Caernarfonshire. He would make her the sole owner and beneficiary. He would not be named … no, wait, he *would* be named, as a person expressly forbidden from inheriting, controlling or otherwise having any interest in the running of that said trust. Then, surely, she would trust him?

Feeling lighter in himself, and confident, he knew what the next step in this personal enterprise should be. He would ensure a dowry for that Miss Waverley. The poor lass had little to recommend her, and from the sounds of things her family had no hope. If he could help get that young woman a husband, it would free him from her, and Amelia would have another successful match for her enterprise.

Drawing up the trust would not be an easy thing. For one, he had to find someone who knew how they worked pertaining to the law. Then he had to find someone willing to do it so that a woman could maintain a business that she had started - and continued to run successfully - without any man's interference, past present or future.

He knew he'd have to read through it. Pain cricked the back of his neck just thinking about that. But he'd do it for Amelia.

The woman who sat politely opposite, a mild expression - not exactly bored, but hardly excitable either - on her face as she gazed out the window.

That's when he hit a mental pot hole. Getting the trust made would mean revealing Miss Remington's identity and her role in said enterprise to a third party without her permission.

He didn't know her all that well, but he knew from the intelligence she displayed and her disposition, that revealing this secret would ruin any future he hoped to share with her.

He would need to develop a better rapport with Miss Remington, in order to gain her trust with the concept of the trust.

The carriage pulled up and they'd arrived. No more ruminating. The footman opened the door and lowered the steps. He exited first and assisted Mrs Lamb and then Miss Remington to alight.

Her hand in his found a natural anchor as she stepped down. Miracle and wonder! She returned his smile and said, "I appreciate the outing, thank you."

"You're most welcome," he beamed back. "You deserve some entertainment, instead of always organising things for others."

Once they were inside, he directed Miss Remington toward a seat. The intention was to sit next to her, but in the blink of an eye, Aunt Lamb took the space beside it. He had to content himself with sitting further over. That Aunt Lamb played the part of a chaperone most convincingly!

The musicale was entertaining. To his ears, the performer was more alto than soprano. He found himself tapping his fingers on his thigh in time with the music. Good singing was good living.

As more people in the audience nodded their heads in appreciation, the relaxed atmosphere and the gestures from the singer encouraged the attendees to join in. No more invitation needed, David's voice joined the performer's and more people joined in.

The mood lifted from polite to lively, and before the next song, it became necessary to move the chairs back to the walls so people had room to dance.

To think, if his ship had been ready on time, he would have missed this.

Those assembled formed lines to dance a reel. A stronger singer than a dancer, David stood up near the musicians (at their encouragement) and joined his voice to theirs once more.

As he looked out across the guests, he saw Miss Remington standing on the sidelines, not dancing. Her face was turned his way, an unreadable expression on her face.

But, if she wasn't dancing, why was she not at least singing?

What was wrong with her?

* * *

Amelia Remington saw the light. How incredibly

inconsiderate of that light to be a series of candles at head-height, shining like a golden halo behind the face of the Marquess of Carnations. She should stop calling him that, it made him far too familiar. As if they were on more friendly terms than they were.

He was the Ardalith of Caernarfonshire and she would do well to remember his station. She was merely Miss Remington, daughter of a gentlewoman, niece to a gentleman's widow.

Yet here she was, at a public gathering, properly chaperoned by said Aunt, who was even now accepting a dance from another gentleman with a thick mop of curled titian hair.

Aunt Lamb? Why was she ... it must only be so that she could appear polite to the man requesting a dance. That had to be why she joined the formation.

As far as Amelia understood, her aunt had not danced since the season where she'd met and married her late husband.

Aunt Lamb danced with her gentleman, a warm and relaxed smile upon her face. This was no case of 'humouring a man until it's over'. Her shoulders were down and her relaxed smile extended to the corners of her eyes.

When the song they were dancing to was over, Amelia turned back to see the marquess bowing politely to the chanteuse, then he looked her way again.

Amelia gulped.

The intensity of his warm gaze caught in her chest and she had to reach for a chair to steady herself. Then he tilted his head towards the ceiling and she followed his eyeline.

Mistletoe.

There was no way she'd go anywhere near that section of the room.

Yet to her surprise, Aunt Lamb and her dancing partner steered straight for it.

Time lost all meaning as Aunt Lamb and her man moved, step by inexorable step, toward that green, weedy kissing trap, hanging over them like a Sword of Damocles.

They were directly under it now.

Aunt Lamb tapped her dance partner on the shoulder and looked up, then turned to him and giggled like a green girl in her first season!

Aunt Lamb!

Her partner made a courteous bow, then reached up and plucked a berry from the plant and placed it in Aunt Lamb's reticule. Then he gently kissed her right on the mouth, in front of everyone!

Amelia gasped. This scandal could destroy their business!

Yet her gasp was ignored by others. Drowned out by the sighs and applause coming from dancers near Aunt Lamb and her paramour. Aunt Lamb curtseyed to him, then they moved away from the Christmas weed to a refreshments table.

The shocks kept coming as more couples steered themselves toward the mistletoe and manufactured a reason to be kissing in public. As each couple reached the greenery, the gentleman took a berry off the plant and gave it to his dance partner. She either accepted it and they kissed, or she let him kiss her gloved hand.

A voice with a familiar burr sounded beside her. "Would you care for a dance?"

"I ... I do not have the required shoes on for dancing. I thought this was a musicale," Amelia replied.

Her breathing wasn't playing fairly in this situation. Drat her overreacting body.

He creased his lips in amusement and said, "I don't think this event has stuck to the script, no. Everyone was sitting still for so long, and the music was so inviting, it seemed the natural thing to do."

How had she let herself be talked in to coming along today? That's right, it had all been the Marquess's suggestion that they come and listen, with an eye to hiring the musicians for future matchmaking evenings. Or at least getting ideas for future events.

The Marquess remained beside her. "If you don't mind me saying, Miss Remington, I did not hear you singing."

"I rarely sing," she said.

"You don't? But … everybody sings."

No, not in public. "In England, women sing in polite company, when they are perhaps hoping to catch the ear and the eye of a gentleman caller."

He made a smirk and looked at her sideways under his lashes. "You do dance, however, don't you?"

"Sometimes."

"There is music and dancing all around you right now, Miss Remington. Would you do me the great honour? I know we came here on business, but that doesn't mean we can't also enjoy ourselves a fraction?"

"I will dance with you, as long as you keep me well away from the mistletoe. And if we happen to be anywhere near it, you will steer me well clear. Is that understood?"

"Completely," he said, offering his hand.

He led her to the impromptu dance floor as the band struck up a reel. Amelia had to laugh at how elegantly the musicians and the singer were dressed, yet the reel required an overdone

Irish accent to sing about a bawdy boy stealing kisses with a fast girl behind a piano.

The thick accent disguised some of the bawdier aspects of the song. It astonished Amelia that the subject of the music could be played in such company! The pace of the dance kept Amelia's thoughts on her next moves, and avoiding the arms of nearby dancers as they swished in and out of formation. It was so energetic, she clear forgot where she was in the room.

The Marquess had better senses than her, and he noticed in time to steer her well away, making it look as if they were simply swapping places with other dancers.

When the dance was over, she applauded the band and the singer, then curtseyed to the Marquess. He bowed to her and indicated they should drink some tea or a lemonade to help them recover.

What a gentleman, to listen to her concerns and follow through with them. She hadn't noticed how close she'd been to that silly bit of greenery. Yet *he* had. Instead of taking advantage of her, he'd steered her away.

He'd listened.

He'd done as she'd requested.

Goodness, he was going to make a wonderful husband to someone one day.

It was a shame she was so against the idea of marriage for herself, because he was the closest anyone had come to make her want to reconsider her deeply held beliefs.

"Have you seen your aunt lately?" he asked, as he filled two cups with tea and handed her one.

Accepting the saucer with the cup balanced on it, Amelia

glanced around the room. "Last I saw she was dancing with that man with the curly orange hair."

"Indeed. The Baron of Abergavenny is hard to miss."

"The Baron of where?"

"Another place in Wales, Abergavenny."

"He's a long way from home, then," Amelia said.

"He is indeed. If only we had some kind of matchmaking service available to us on our side of the Wye River, we wouldn't be filling up your houses here."

Amelia chuckled at his cheekiness and sipped her tea. She liked listening to him talk, but his singing voice had been a revelation. It would be too much to ask him to sing for her. Far too intimate. But all the same she wanted to hear him sing again.

Soon.

* * *

David enjoyed the sound of Amelia's laugh. He was sure he would enjoy the sound of her singing as well, if she ever sang for him. A girl that didn't sing was like a bird that didn't fly.

He was glad he'd been able to spot the mistletoe in time. He didn't have any time for superstitions and cornering people into kissing. If a girl didn't want to kiss you, then she didn't need a reason. And he knew, from watching the behaviour of his own extended family back home, if a girl wanted a kiss, she would let you know. None of this dilly dallying about.

Didn't mean he wasn't thinking about kissing Miss Amelia Remington every minute of his waking hours, and most of his sleeping ones too.

Her widowed aunt, however, was another matter. Perhaps having the excuse that she was a widow, rather than a blushing debutante, she could kiss whomever she chose?

Aunt Lamb and Abergavenny had kissed each other without a care in the world, despite their audience, and now it was clear to David that the two of them had gone somewhere where they would *not* have an audience.

Abergavenny was a decent sort, as far as David knew. His family had never had troubles from them, and had never given it. He wasn't keen on the way they'd turned over most of their pastoral lands to coal mines, but ultimately that was Abergavenny's choice.

It also meant the coal miners moving to the area needed to eat, which created an opportunity for David and others who still had enough land to grow food to feed those miners.

His eyes came to rest on Miss Remington. "I don't mean to worry you at all, but where is your aunt Lamb?"

"I'm right behind you," her familiar voice announced.

Caernarfonshire and Amelia turned at the same time to see Aunt Lamb holding hands with the Baron of Abergavenny.

Aunt Lamb made the introductions. "My Lord Caernarfonshire, this is the Baron of Abergavenny, and this is my niece, Miss Remington."

The Baron shook David's hand, then made a polite bow over Amelia's and said, "Caernarfonshire, Miss Remington, I'm delighted to make your acquaintance. Miss Remington, it is my singular honour as Mrs Lamb's closest relative to ask your permission that we marry."

David nearly swallowed his tongue in shock. The Baron sure did move quickly.

* * *

The request sent a bolt of surprise through Amelia. "My permission?"

"Yes." The Baron beamed. The man looked so filled with admiration for her aunt, how could she refuse?

It was all so fast.

The Baron took her hesitance as a chance to explain himself further. "I have asked for her hand, and she has accepted. As her family is no longer with us, the privilege of permission falls to your good self."

She'd better say something quickly, this was so terribly awkward. "My Lord, ah, My Aunt is a wonderful woman, and as my elder and a widow long out of mourning, she is completely capable of making her own decisions." Amelia stunned herself with how articulate she sounded through her reverberating shock.

This was all so sudden!

Had Aunt Lamb known Abergavenny would be here? That might explain why they spent so much time dancing, and why she'd agreed so readily to the Marquess's invitation to come.

They were still looking at her, waiting for her acceptance. "You do not need my permission, but you have it anyway."

She could hardly refuse.

"Thank you, my dear," Aunt Lamb said, embracing her niece in a fierce hug. "George and I were acquainted many years ago, and we are delighted to have found each other once again."

From the speed of things, they'd been much more than *acquainted*, but Amelia let that thought pass as she took in the happiness on her aunt's face, and the Baron's.

Goodness, her aunt was going to be a Baroness!

What a fabulous match. How excellent this would be for their matchmaking business.

And then, as they congratulated each other and shared more

hugs and Amelia gave the Baron a kiss on his cheek to welcome him into the family, he went and destroyed everything with his next statement.

"Your aunt has told me about the enterprise she has been running, and how sad she will be to give that up to become the Baroness of Abergavenny. We shall welcome you to our home, you would be most welcome to come and live with us, especially if my new wife has children."

Impotent confusion filled Amelia. The baron honestly thought he was saying the right thing? The patronising fool.

She was the one running the whole enterprise! Aunt Lamb was just the face of it. And now she was toddling off to marry her sweetheart, and possibly have his heirs, and they were offering her … *charity*?

Amelia smiled as politely as she could manage. "This is all such lovely and wonderful news. I could not possibly come and live with you right away, as you have so many years to catch up on. I will be perfectly fine here."

"You are being far too polite," he said, "I insist you come and live with us. I am so lucky to have found my lost lamb, I must extend my hospitality to you."

How did she get out of this mess?

She needed to speak to the Baron and explain the true nature of their enterprise. Once he understood, all would be well.

As long as she could trust him.

Her chances of getting his undivided attention, when he only had eyes for Aunt Lamb, were slim. Her head swam with her pulse as the Baron mentioned how he'd be obtaining a special licence so "my lamb and I can marry as soon as possible."

As soon as they arrived in Abergavenny, apparently. Three days by carriage, if the weather was amenable.

6

The next few days were a flurry of preparations and packing to move. The Baron talked of selling Aunt Lamb's London home to consolidate their estates.

Every day closer to departure meant a day closer to losing her future. Before now, Amelia's worst fear was that she might end up having to marry and lose everything. Which is why she'd steadfastly refused to do so. She hadn't counted on her aunt remarrying and making that decision to close the enterprise for her.

She found George in the hall, directing staff who were taking trunks ahead of them to his estate in Abergavenny.

"My Lord, may I have an audience?"

"My dear Miss Remington, you may always speak freely to me. But we shall have to conduct the conversation here as I direct which carriage each trunk must go to."

"Thank you," she was thankful, truly, but also very fearful. "Would it be so bad if I remained here in London?"

He blanched.

"Just for a little longer, in order to uh … have time to farewell my friends."

"Oh goodness me no, you may invite as many friends as you need to come visit in Abergavenny. My home shall be yours. But for you to remain here? I could not, in all good conscience, allow that. An unchaperoned woman, living alone? It simply cannot be done."

"I have staff –"

"– Please, Miss Remington, all will be well. I can understand your nerves about relocating, but you will adore Wales, and Abergavenny especially. It is God's own country."

Amelia forced a smile and knew she'd lost. Everything she had suspected about marriage was coming true. The moment a woman married, her husband controlled everything!

She thanked the baron and retreated to her writing desk, where she assessed the voluminous correspondence. The Baron had not approved of her handling 'men's work', but she'd left him in the hall directing the staff, so he would not bother her.

Later, they would be rugged up against the beastly weather and take a walk, or perhaps a ride through the park with some blankets, so they could accept the congratulations of everyone they met along the way.

The correspondence was full of congratulations for Aunt Lamb's dazzling success, with her betrothal to a Baron. Alas, each congratulatory message also bore condolences for the necessary ending of the enterprise.

Worse than that, some were asking if their remaining

vouchers could be transferred to another business? Some were even asking for a complete refund.

Running away to Abergavenny might have its advantages after all, if their clients were chasing them for funds.

Amelia replied to each person, thanking them for their good wishes and did not reply further. She had no way of knowing how her business was to proceed from here, but it wasn't looking positive. Especially as she hadn't been able to speak about the matter with the Baron in any detail. Did he even know Aunt Lamb was only the public face of their enterprise, and that it had been Amelia's idea - and toil - all along?

Amelia sighed and finished her correspondence. Their next, and possibly final soirée was in two evenings' time. Yet another strain on Amelia's nerves.

An idea burst forth to explain to the Baron the sudden appearance of eligible men and women at the house. Amelia and Aunt Lamb would pretend those arriving were there to congratulate the happy couple on their connection. Amelia would repurpose the event as a supper in the Baron and Aunt Lamb's honour. She would continue the matchmaking while the Baron and Aunt Lamb were distracted with so many people wishing them well.

Oh goodness, it all sounded so achievable, Amelia wondered why she hadn't thought of it before. Possibly the emotions roiling through her, the uncertainty of what her new life involved. Metaphorical storms had robbed her of clear sky thinking.

A smile grew as she knew exactly what to add to all those letters she'd replied to. Thank goodness she hadn't sealed them.

At the bottom of each, she wrote, *"Please come at 4pm on Tuesday afternoon to congratulate the betrothed couple."*

No word of whether this would be their last event, and there wasn't room on the paper at any rate.

Satisfied she'd be able to explain everything (and satisfy their hunger for refunds, which they would *not* be getting) Amelia took a fresh leaf of paper, screwed up her courage and wrote the words she never thought she would ever commit.

Dear Marquess of Caernarfonshire,

I accept your offer of marriage.

Please visit at my home to gain permission from the new head of our household, the Baron of Abergavenny.

Yours, Amelia Remington.

It took several breaths before she could bring herself to fold the letter, address it and seal it, then she added it to the top of the pile and gave the entire bundle to the footman.

Once he'd left the house, Amelia was alone - as alone as anyone could be with a butler and cook and other staff about the house. But she was alone as she'd been since ... since she could ever remember. She'd come to live with Aunt Lamb long before her mother had died.

Sitting by the fire that afternoon, Amelia's needlework was not behaving. The thread twisted beneath the hoop and caught itself in knots. It slipped from her hand and when she picked it up, both sides looked so equally messy, she wasn't sure which was supposed to face up.

She dropped it into her sewing basket and slumped over to the piano forte. She had her notebook where she'd copied out some tunes, and sat down to play. Her fingers were cool and messy to begin with, but as long as she didn't think about things too much, they warmed and eventually found the correct keys. The tune pleased her ear.

Before long she sang the melody, a playful ditty about a girl getting a posy of flowers from a handsome admirer. The more she played, the more she sang, until another smooth baritone voice joined in.

She looked up and clanged the keys in shock.

The Marquess of Caernarfonshire stood there, holding a posy of hothouse flowers.

"So, you do sing!" He beamed, stepping closer to her and pressing the flowers towards her. "Don't stop on my account, you play beautifully, and your singing is grand."

"I did not hear you come in, My Lord!"

"The butler gave me entrance, and I followed the sound. You have a delightful voice."

Goodness, she'd forgotten her manners. Standing up from the instrument, she came towards him and delivered a quick curtsey, then accepted the flowers. "I'll get the m-"

She'd been about to say 'maid', but the maid had appeared near the doorway to take the flowers and put them in a vase.

The Marquess cleared his throat and said, "I received your letter. Your change of heart has surely gladdened mine."

She had to remember to breathe. "I have indeed had a change of heart."

He reached for her hand and she gave it, then he guided them to sit on the chaise, not completely close together, but within reaching distance.

"Dare I ask what brought it about?"

She looked into his beautiful eyes and blurted, "I have no other avenues available to me."

7

I f David had been slapped with a cold rag, her words could not have chilled him more. It was hardly the declaration of affection he'd been hoping for. Then again, he'd made such a hash of their first meeting, he could hardly expect her to come around so quickly.

But she could have said she'd begun to form some kind of affection, surely?

"I must apologise," she said, as if suddenly aware of the brutality of her words. "That is not what I intended to say."

"But maybe it's the truth? What's made such a change?" If they were going to marry, then he really should know why. He felt sure this would lead to a better outcome for both of them if they were honest about their reasons for this alliance. As the thought grew in his mind, he understood he should be honest with her, too, about why he'd formed such a fast attachment.

She swallowed and said, "You are a charming man, and I am able to converse reasonably easily with you."

He was breathing again, that was a good sign. He wasn't sure how much his heart could take of this. "That's good to know. I'd like a wife who is able to carry on a conversation with me. I like to talk."

He tried to make light of things, but she didn't seem all that happy. The way her mouth turned down at the ends. The way the light was missing from her eyes. Her hand was still in his, so he gently rubbed her knuckles with his thumb, encouraging her to free her heart.

At the same time, his heart constricted. This was not the meeting of souls he had anticipated on his journey to England. He wanted to return with a wife, not a prisoner.

She swallowed again and her voice came out thin as a reed. "As you witnessed the other day, the Baron and Aunt Lamb have formed an attachment. Or, more accurately, they have reignited an old tendre. They are to leave for Abergavenny in a few days. But as he is to be the head of the household, I must leave with them. That means leaving the enterprise as well."

No other avenues indeed! "I take it you don't really want to go, do you?"

She pressed her lips together, then licked the dryness away. The action of her pink tongue on her lips sent a jolt of lust through his body.

"You have read me like a book, My Lord," she explained. "I do not wish to leave London, I do not wish to give up my independence or the business. It was ... it *is* ... something that I am quite accomplished in. We have made three good matches this season already, and I know from the calling card exchanges after our last soirée, there will be more in the new year. It has grown to be quite the success."

"The Baron doesn't know, does he?"

Amelia slumped. "He knows a little, but he doesn't know all. He's encouraged Aunt Lamb to stop, and she sees no reason to keep going now that she has found her love. I do not want to come between their affections. If my aunt has rekindled an old flame, she should be free to do so."

He needed to say something to show he was listening, even though his heart was beating far too quickly. "Quite the pickle, isn't it?"

Flog him for being a fool, that was a morose thing to say given the circumstances!

"It has always been my endeavour, and Aunt Lamb played her part. I think she enjoyed it, and it made use of her widowhood and position … I know that left to my own devices, I *could* keep going. But without Aunt Lamb here with me, we lose our public face. Nobody would trust an unwed woman to run such an enterprise."

It was a terrible bind. "Perception is everything, is it not?"

"It is."

"And so, your only two options are to leave with your aunt and the Baron, or take your chances with marrying me?" Saying it out aloud did not make it any less brutal.

She dabbed a handkerchief to her nose and said, "If you will have me."

Not the ringing endorsement he was after. Still, it was a starting place. Perhaps more than a start? "What if there was a way to keep the enterprise running?"

She dabbed at her face and looked to him. "Do you mean I sell the business?"

"No, you would keep it and still run it. Because it brings you joy, and you are good at it."

She pulled back and seemed confused. "You're that confident I could keep it going, as an unmarried woman in society?"

Not quite. "Please, don't misunderstand me. We'd still marry, but I'd put everything into a legal trust arrangement, so you get to keep everything and control all of it. I would legally have no interest and no claim at all."

"I don't suppose there's a way I can keep the supper soirées going and not have to marry you?"

Oof, what a deep blow to his ego. "Well," he took a breath to get past the emotional rejection, "Your marriage to me would mean you'd outrank the Baron, and with such a successful marriage … it would mean you'd become a society matron. It could even place you in a better position, and also advertise the incredible success of your enterprise."

She burst into tears at that and collapsed face-first onto the cushions.

Not the result he was looking for. "Is that really such a horrible concept?"

"No," she sniffed, "It's absolutely marvellous," she blew her nose heavily. "Why are you being so nice to me?"

"Because I want a happy wife!" Wasn't that obvious? "If you're miserable, I'd be miserable too. Why should we both be miserable? I'll not have that."

* * *

It took a while for his words - and the true meaning of them - to permeate her mood. He wanted a happy wife?

In all her months of matchmaking, in all the time looking through people's required and desirable qualities they were looking for, how often had people mentioned a requirement that the other person be happy?

It pained her to realise some people had mentioned how happy *they* would be to find a husband or a wife, but that was very different.

"That is," she struggled to find the words, "An unusual proposition. That you want me to be happy."

"Have I grown a second head?" He asked, blinking a few times at the thought. Then he touched his neck, left and right, to make a show of his search. "I would have thought every man would want a happy wife, just as every woman would want a happy husband?"

Amelia breathed through the surprise of it all. It's true he had blundered his first impression. He'd not seemed the least bit fussy about whom he married. Yet now he was admitting he valued her happiness, to ensure his own. "It is not something any gentleman has declared when listing the qualities of a future wife."

He creased his brow. "You mean, in all this time arranging marriages, nobody has mentioned the other's moods?"

A large sigh. "Not so much. They … I guess I'm giving away all my business secrets now, but the gentlemen only want a certain … disposition. They tend to ask for a quiet, accomplished young woman who will make a good mother and biddable wife. They speak of how this will contribute to their own happiness, of course."

"And what do the ladies want?"

Ah yes, the ladies. "If they are truly honest, they are after a title, if at all possible. Failing that, somebody who may later inherit a title, or a gentleman of means, to ensure a comfortable life."

"And they don't care about his disposition?"

"They do," Amelia corrected. "Nobody wants a brute, but it's very hard to know if that's what they will turn into, once they are married. I've heard it can happen if the wife does not adjust easily to her new place in the world."

He shook his head. "You mean the men are putting on an act to secure a wife, then once they're married, the curtain falls and their true natures are free once more."

Amelia took a deep breath. "I certainly hope that is never the case. I do keep correspondence with my customers and none have indicated any sudden changes in demeanour. I am very grateful for that, at least. I think Aunt Lamb has been incredibly judicious in that regard, sniffing out the cads ahead of time."

He made a low chortle. "This is me you're talking to, I know Aunt Lamb is the show pony, but you're the true workhorse, getting things done."

"Being compared to an equine is not the flattery you think it is!" Moments ago, he'd mentioned that her happiness was paramount, now he was comparing her to livestock? Did the man not have any manners?

"That's because I wasn't trying to flatter you. I was making an apt comparison to recognise how hard you work. In some ways, you work hard to make sure everyone else is happy, and don't think about your own needs."

"An excellent recovery," she said with a rueful tone.

"Oh, I think you are a workhorse, and you get the job done, and you're unseen by everyone else who gets to enjoy the fruits of your labours. Now, if you're after flattery, I can tell you I don't throw it around for the sake of it. However, it does please me to see you smile. It's like a candle in the darkness, the way it lights up your whole face. It's good to see you shining."

Heat spread through her at his words. He seemed the kind of person who did as he said - he wasn't one for handing out compliments easily, but she felt she'd earned this rare bon mot from him. That made it all the more valuable. Something in that warmth sparkled inside her, at the thought of earning more compliments from him.

Goodness, what was he doing to her?

She'd stopped crying properly now, and no longer needed her handkerchief. "I must admit, I am pleased someone has noticed how much work I have put in to this enterprise. Aunt Lamb has enjoyed her exalted position, but aside from that, she does not truly understand what I do. I don't think anyone does, really."

"Is this why it hurts so much that she's accepted Abergavenny and expects you to follow?"

Amelia nodded. How did he see her so clearly? "Her upcoming wedding to the Baron is the talk of society. There are a few who think she was hiding his presence so she could keep him to herself, but ultimately it was his choice to propose. In any other situation, if there were a man at the helm of this enterprise, it would be seen as proof we were the best matchmakers in the ton. Alas, the success has come at the price of having to end the enterprise. She has no interest in remaining in London, much less keep up the pretence."

He was quiet for a while, as he ruminated and worried his top lip, as if chewing something invisible. After a time he said, "A maiden is not seen as fit and proper person to run such a matchmaking scheme. Society would be more amenable to … I'm clutching at straws here to be honest … a Marquess as the face of the enterprise?"

Amelia was not given to fainting, but she felt liable to swoon. "You'd do that for me?"

"I would, if you'd marry me."

Lost for words, again, Amelia blurted, "This is all so sudden."

"No it's not. It's about the fifth time I've asked you, surely you're getting used to it by now?"

He had her there.

"There are a great many things I am worried about," Amelia confessed. "Not the business, which I think we could run together very well, if you were the public face of it. But marriage is … it terrifies me. I need to be honest and I can't be happy until I speak my truth. I don't want to die in childbirth, as seems to happen with alarming regularity."

The colour drained from his face.

Amelia pressed on, "I know mothers often have to bury their children who don't make it, as evidenced by the headstones in the church graveyard. And also … ah … the thought of what might need to be done to have those children does confuse and scare me, because I can only go by what Aunt Lamb tells me that it is something to be endured. Mind you, Aunt Lamb is besotted with the Baron, so perhaps she is up for some endurance after all?"

Amelia finally stopped, but her heartbeat and her breathing raced onwards.

The Marquess said, "I can only say that I will be there for you. I hope I don't die in childbirth myself."

"You? How would you die?"

"I'll faint and smack my head and leave you a widow with a screaming babi."

Laughter burst forth. "I'm being silly, aren't I?"

"Naw, you're being honest and I like that. I'm a little scared too. I hope none of those things happen. We don't know what the good Lord has in store for us. That's why we need to take our chances when we can. And be as happy as we can for the time we have."

He was so reassuring and reasonable about all of it. "There is one other complication. This house is Aunt Lamb's and it will soon belong to the Baron. How am I to host the soirees without a residence?"

He nodded and thought for a moment, then said, "I could buy it from him, would that work?"

"That's ... incredibly generous of you." It might even lead to a genuine bout of swooning if she wasn't careful. "You would do that for me? A woman you barely know. It's a huge financial risk to do that, knowing you would have no controlling interest after the trust is drawn up."

"My interest is in having a happy wife, who, from what I have already attested, is incredibly clever. It would be a bigger risk to take you away from all this and drag you off to Caernarfonshire, where you'd probably be miserable at having to give up your successful enterprise."

She really was starting to like him rather a lot. But something still niggled. "At some point, you would want me to be in Caernarfonshire, with you, as your Marchioness. Correct?"

"Yes. I thought it would be best if we lived in London for the season, then travelled to Wales for the summer. The climate will be far more pleasant. Am I to understand there is not so much matchmaking in the summer, at least in London?"

"That ... is true. Most society families go to their country estates, and parliament is closed." Goodness, he'd thought of everything.

He gave a smile, as if something delighted him. "In the summer, society ladies host house parties at their country estates, do they not? Could you carry on the same kind of enterprise in Wales? We have dozens of eligible ladies and gentlemen that need introductions and a guiding hand to make good matches."

"Does that mean you'd stay here in London, with me, for the rest of the winter?"

"Well, yes, but only as husband and wife. It would be an enormous scandal if I was living here and you were unwed and unchaperoned, with a dashing Marquess living under the same roof."

Amelia burst out laughing.

"Does that mean you will marry me?"

Was that the sixth time he'd asked?

A wicked thought tickled Amelia's mind. "I guess I'd better then, but only in order to prevent a *terrible scandal* that would ruin my business."

"Will you ever flatter me, simply to make me feel better?" heasked, taking her hand in his and kissing her palm.

Sparks shot through her system, and she teased him a little more. "I will flatter you when it's the truth," she said.

"May I kiss you?"

She had agreed to marry him. It made sense to get the kissing done and out of the way. The other parts of marriage would be dealt with in due time. But he'd promised she could keep running her soirées and keep living in Aunt Lamb's house at least for this season. She could endure a kiss for that. "Yes, you may."

He gave a lopsided, happy smile, then leaned in and brushed her lips, feather-light, with his own. It was so fast and ethereal, she could have imagined it. It wasn't anything terrifying or demanding at all, in fact it was -

He kissed her again, more firmly this time, and something flipped behind her ribs. She pulled back. "I'm sorry."

He blinked. "What are you sorry for?"

"Something is wrong with me. My heart just cramped or something. I may be sickening."

"Oh dear," he studied her face, then kissed her again.

Her heart did that flip again. She pulled back, "Am I unwell all of a sudden? This is most unusual."

"I believe I recognise the cause, for my blood is quickening too," he confessed. "When you kiss me, my pulse hammers in my ears."

"Is this ... normal?"

"Apparently," he said. "But we shall have to keep kissing, just to make sure."

This time she leaned forwards and pressed her lips to his. Something heavy thrummed in her system. She placed her hands gently on either side of his face and held him closer. It was the most deliciously dangerous thing she'd ever experienced, and she wanted more. He showed no signs of pulling away, so she kept on kissing. Her mouth opened on a breath and he did the same, swooning and sighing as he opened his lips for her.

It was divine!

Breath coming faster, Amelia eventually pulled away and

rested her forehead on his. "Is this what being married is like? I begin to understand the appeal now."

"Apparently there's more," he said.

She pulled back. "More?"

"So I've been told, although I've yet to experience it. I'm sure we'll manage, somehow."

"At the risk of flattering you far too early in the relationship, your kisses have quite turned my head."

He smiled warmly, with a touch of wicked. "I have few kisses to compare to ours, but yours have quite blown the milk off my tea."

Amelia covered her mouth to stop from laughing too loudly.

"Ah, see, I made you laugh and enjoy a good kiss. Surely that's a good quality in a future husband?"

Still smiling, but gaining her equilibrium, Amelia tilted her head to the side. "I feel it is incumbent on me to warn you, I might make a terrible wife."

"In what ways?"

Plural? Oh, he was good!

"In so many ways." She ticked imaginary poor qualities off her fingers. "I am headstrong and want to get my own way far too much. I covet my own company. I like to organise things myself, and not be organised by others. And … worst of all, I like making money, all by myself."

He grinned like a wolf. "They are all excellent qualities."

"In a man perhaps, but don't you feel it is unnatural?"

"What is unnatural about wanting to make a good living? And as far as I can tell, you've been doing just that, and hardly anyone has noticed in all this time."

"Except you."

"Well, I notice things, you see. I notice that society puts a great deal of weight on people having money, but they don't like to know how you actually make it. You have found the perfect solution. I would barely have to provide for you at all. I'm gaining a wife who is clever and understands people, who is resourceful and good with figures. In time, I hope we both get children out of it. Who knows, we might even like some of them!"

Laughter burst free. "Go on!" Amelia gave up trying to stop the chortling. Oh goodness, she was going to get married! "Is there anything you think I should know, before it's too late to change our minds?"

"I would want our children to speak Welsh and English, if that's all the same with you."

Amelia nodded. It seemed a mild request, and something that could be useful.

He added, "We should live in London during the season, and move to my estate for the rest of the yor."

She loved the way he said that.

He had quite the list. "I should like your advice on various matters, when they arise. You have a sharp mind, I want to avail myself of it."

That brought her up short. "What sort of matters?"

"Crop rotations, estate management, animal management. We mostly grow wheat and barley, but I know if you put your mind to it, you could find a way to make that more lucrative."

A scoff formed, but Amelia held it down. "I'm not sure how much help I could be, but I will do my best to understand the situation, when the season is over."

"One more thing. I should like your help with reading."

She was stunned into silence for a moment and could only blink.

"To my great shame, I'm not very good at it. I get a headache when I try, so I try not to, as much as possible." He looked at her, his palms flickered upwards in defeat, waiting for her approbation.

Realisation hit Amelia. "That's why you offered for me so quickly!" It all made sense now. When he'd walked in - it wasn't that he didn't respect their proper hours of business, it was that he hadn't read them. He'd offered for her hand immediately because he could tell by the paperwork in her hands that she could read.

"It is I who must apologise to you," Amelia said. "Why do we not get you some spectacles and see if they make a difference? Aunt Lamb barely writes any more, she dictates to me as she says her joints stiffen, especially in winter. She uses a lorgnette to read the news sheets."

"They are such an affectation, I tried one but it made me look like a preening peacock." He scoffed. "I thought you might ridicule me."

"Why would I do that? There's no shame in needing spectacles. I'm sure I shall need some of my own before long."

"And do spectacles stop the letters from swapping over?"

"What?"

"The letters sometimes swap over, so I end up … wuddling my merds."

Amelia pressed her lips together so she would not laugh. "I shall maintain your discretion, and help whenever you require."

He let out a sigh of relief, as if the very issue had been nibbling away at him like a mouse at a block of cheese.

8

The farewell and betrothal party for Aunt Lamb and Baron Abergavenny was turning into quite the crush. It may have been a few days before Christmas, the wind may have blown the feathers off a barn owl, but the guests ignored all of this to arrive at the afternoon soirée. As if the very walls bowed to the sides as people poured from room to room. Some rooms were filled with chair lining the walls, the carpets earlier rolled up to make room for dancing. Other rooms were more of the cosy variety, the fire keeping the room well-lit with light and warmth, and the candles in the lanterns along the walls were casting flickering shadows.

They'd never had such a fabulous turnout. Yes, the reason was for people to wish the newly betrothed couple well on their new life together, but for Amelia, it was still work. She mental checked off each arrival against the register, and handed out the dance cards and pencils, and also pencils for the gentlemen to write the names of debutantes with whom they'd like to become better acquainted on the back.

People everywhere. Sparkling eyes, happy smiles, gentlemen sneaking their calling cards into women's reticules when they thought nobody would see them. Amelia saw it all, and swelled with pride. What a fabulous turnout.

What a marvellous opportunity to make even more matches and hold more celebrations into the new year. Everything was going to fabulously well.

Until the speeches.

Everyone had gathered into the largest of the front rooms, but there was not enough space so the guests spilled into the hall and stairs, ears strained to hear everything the happy couple were saying.

"Thank you all ever so, for your good cheer," The Baron said. Aunt lamb smiled beatifically at her paramour. "I have found my lost lamb after all these years, and I am the happiest man in the world that she will soon be my baroness."

He paused and people cheered their good wishes.

"I'm sure she's had a wonderful impact on your lives to date, but now you will understand it is time for my dear Lamb to hang up her match-making days as she begins a new chapter in her life, with me!"

More applause and cheers filled the house. Of course everyone would understand that Aunt Lamb would not be matchmaking in the immediate sense. But had he meant to make it sound so final? That there would never be any more of the enterprise?

Pleadingly, she looked to the Marquess to say a few words.

He mildly cleared his throat and wished his felicitations to the bride and groom, "But fear not, the enterprise will continue. I have bought this very property from the good Baron, and in the new yor we shall have more soirées and dances and musical entertainments."

That brought a round of polite applause, but not the great cheers Amelia expected.

"I say, good sir," one of the eligible gentlemen guests suggested, "I hardly think it will be the same without Aunt Lamb. She was the heart and soul of the house. She's impossible to replace."

The bottom fell out of Amelia's world. It had been all her hard work!

"Ah, but you see," the Marquess continued, "We shall have continuity. Young Amelia here will still be directly involved."

Someone coughed.

One of the society matrons, oh look, it was Mrs Waverley, suggested, "An unmarried woman making such important decisions? I hardly believe my ears."

"But she's not unmarried." The Marquess said, "at least, not for long. I've asked her to become my wife and she's accepted."

If a sinkhole opened directly under the house, it could hardly be less disruptive. Amelia felt the full attention of all eyes on her. People peered in from the hallway, as whispered susurrations rippled around the room and then out to those in the hall and on the stairs.

David held out his hand to Amelia and she had no option but to step forward and accept it. In doing so, she said, "We did not mean to take any attention from your party, Aunt Lamb, truly we did not."

Aunt Lamb pulled Amelia into an embrace and said, "I'm

delighted for you." Then she took advantage of a lull in the room and said, "My niece to a Marquess! The best match I could ever have made, and one I doubt even I could ever best."

A cacophony broke out as people cheered and applauded all the more.

The Baron had to yell to be heard, "Let's have a toast to London's finest matchmaker, The Baroness." He held his glass aloft. "To The Baroness!"

Everyone responded to the call: "The Baroness!"

Oh hell!

As each guest departed, they curtseyed to the Baron and kissed Aunt Lamb. All said variations of, "The London Season won't be the same without you." Killing off any sentiment people had for anyone associated with the house, or Amelia.

By claiming to have made the match, Aunt Lamb had unwittingly sunk Amelia's hopes of continuing the enterprise, even with her husband, a Marquess, at the helm.

As the hired staff cleared the rooms away and rolled the carpets back into place, David approached her. "I'm sorry the guests took all of this the wrong way."

Amelia sighed. "I did far too good a job of making them believe it was all Aunt Lamb's doing."

"That you did. I spent the rest of the evening trying to convince the gentlemen that I would be an excellent business partner, but they wouldn't have it. Even though I said you'd be doing the work, and a married woman would be the perfect person. They were saying they felt sorry for me that the wife of a Marquess would have to work. They suggested in rather mild tones that I was a fraud."

"Oh dear."

"Unfortunately, I have come to the conclusions that appearances count more for most people than skills."

"That is about right."

"You don't have to marry me, if you've changed your mind."

"What?" She'd lost her business, her home, and now her almost-husband? "Do you want to throw me over?"

"Not in the slightest, but … you don't have to marry me anymore because the reason isn't really there … and in any case, you'd have more success if you became a widow."

"Don't say such things!"

He looked crestfallen. "I've messed everything up for you. I thought I was offering you a way though, but I've ruined the lot."

"Stop that. You didn't ruin anything. It occurs to me that Aunt Lamb and I got away with things for as long as we could, but it would have fallen apart at some point. We started the enterprise because we were in need of funds, and this was an acceptable trade we could engage in. Now that everyone publicly thinks it was all Lamb, and she's marrying a Baron, well, that neatly concludes her business."

"But yours is not finished, you will go spare with nothing to occupy you."

"I will still marry you, Marquess, if you'll have me. An utter nobody tainted by trade."

"Yes please," he reached for her hand and kissed it, then looked at her from under his lashes, "May I have a proper kiss?"

"Excellent idea."

They kissed in the cool night air, a focus of heat on their lips as they gave each other comfort and promises of things to come. When they stopped, their breaths appeared in foggy spurts.

"I've had an idea," Amelia began. "The sale went through, so you own the property here."

"I do. And thank you for reading through the contract, I had a headache before reaching half way through the first page."

"I was glad to help. Now, how does this sound. We go to your estate in Caernarfonshire and do what married people do for a while, running the estate and all that."

"I like the sound of that."

"And then later, during next season, we could perhaps start again."

"But people would remember you? It seems it would be impossible to take up where you left off."

"Ahhhh, but this is the clever part. We use a different name. I install a genteel widow as the public face of it all."

He smiled in conspiracy with her, "I love how clever you are?"

She kissed him again with all the love she had in her. When she pulled back, she asked, "I don't suppose you know any genteel widows by any chance? Ones that aren't likely to rush off and marry a childhood sweetheart any time soon?"

He pulled back and scratched his head. "Well, my mother's a widow, that's why I'm the Marquess."

"Perfect!" Amelia kissed him again and quite forgot about

the cold weather. "Do you think she'd be interested in being the face of an enterprise like this?"

"I wouldn't possibly answer on her behalf. But you're welcome to ask, when you meet her."

Amelia grinned at the possibilities. A dowager Marchioness as a match-maker. How perfect!

EPILOGUE

After their wedding, they stopped at many inns in many towns on the way to Caernarfonshire. They spent each night together, getting to know each other, learning what pleased the other and themselves.

"I must apologise," she said as they sat in the carriage on the last section of their journey. "I was wrong about marriage."

"You're not wrong about every marriage, some of them are truly hideous, so I've heard," he said. "Ours could still sour."

She elbowed him in the ribs. "Don't say that!"

"You may soon tire of me, wanting you to read contract after contract, and constantly asking your opinion about how to run things."

"What else would I do at any rate?"

"I don't know. Be a Marchioness and take tea with visitors."

Amelia laughed. "That would sour me quickly. Oh dear. Turn the carriage around, I've made a terrible mistake!"

He grabbed her and kissed her thoroughly. "Too late now."

"Too late for you too."

* * *

They met the staff, and the marquess showed her around the estate. Soon they paid a visit to the dower house, and Amelia and her mother-in-law sipped tea and talked about the weather.

"You might think this is a little mad, my Lady. But, how do you feel about match making?"

"Oh, I rather enjoy it," the Dowager Marchioness said. "Whom do you have in mind?"

"Let's refill our tea," Amelia said as she signalled to the maid to refresh her cup. "I need to tell you how your son and I met. It was through a matchmaker, and it's given me an idea for a rather wonderful enterprise."

Her mother-in-law cast Amelia a sly grin. "An Ardalythes should not be working, unless it's for her estate."

"Ah yes, I completely agree. However, a widow would be the perfect person to entrust young debutantes and eligible gentlemen with the marriage market, do you not agree?"

"You've had a good while to think about this, it's a week by carriage to London from here."

Truth be told, Amelia hadn't had much time to think on the journey, this was all decided before they left London, but it was nice of her mother-in-law to spare her blushes. "I shan't burden you with too much for now, but it's something I'd like to resume. David has let our London house for the rest of the season and we shan't be needing it for the immediate future.

"No, I suspect you'll want to focus on the nursery."

Chills of fear dropped hard in Amelia's stomach. A nursery.

"Are you all right, dear?"

"I'm sorry, I … I hadn't thought about that. I have no concept of what is involved. I shall need your advice for that as well."

"I would be delighted to help. It's a fair way off in any case."

"Is it?"

"Did your mother not educate you?"

"Ahhh, she died when I was young, and I have lived with my widowed aunt whose husband died only a few months after they were wed. To be honest, I don't think she liked him very much, as she always held a tendre for the Baron of Abergavenny, to whom she is now wed."

The dowager put down her cup. "Ahhhh, she's the long-lost love I've heard about."

"You've heard about the Baron already?"

"Oh yes, I know all the nobles on this side of the Wye."

Amelia snickered as she sipped more tea. "And how many of them need a good match?"

"Quite a few."

That sparked fresh ideas. "Perhaps we don't need to wait to return to London, perhaps we could begin an enterprise here?"

"I think you and I are going to get along famously. Welcome to the family, my dear. Call me Mam."

I adore David and Amelia, and I hope you do too. They have a cameo in *Marriage, She Wrote*. Turn the page for a sneak peek of that sweet romance

MARRIAGE, SHE WROTE

PROLOGUE

February 1816
February 16
Bangor Hall

*D*earest Mama,

This is a dreadful state of affairs. I did no wrong. I was on my way to wed the gallant Captain Tenby. The Captain said the anvil was mere hours away when our axle broke. That's not my fault. You cannot blame me for something that was completely out of my control. The weather has been dreadful across the entire country, apparently. As an aside, I cannot wait for summer, so we can see an end to this hideous gloom.

I repeat my point, none of this is my fault. Falling in love is completely natural. You said so yourself. Why has Papa sent me so far away? Why not simply bring me home where I can explain all? I now find myself in the middle of nowhere. This is most unfair.

The moment Captain Tenby and I are together again, we shall wed, you will see. Then all will be well.

Your darling Demeter

March 2,
Penrose House,
Bath

Dear Demeter,

I have only today received your letter and hope this does not take as long to reach you as your missive took to reach me. The fact of the matter is you remain unwed. Eloping is enough of a scandal, but failing to elope has brought unspeakable shame on us all. The fact is, no matter your intentions, your carriage never made it to Gretna Green. Your 'wonderful captain' has not returned.

We have also heard rumors that he may not be all he claims.

Can you truly not appreciate how much your actions have brought the whole family low? Especially your sisters, whose very seasons in London are at risk! I am also punished in that I must remain in Bath under the appearances of taking the waters for my nerves. I am even further in my brother's debt as his wife has agreed to chaperone Persephone and Hestia for their season. We can only hope that people do not make the connection between my brother and his wayward niece. You must remain where you are, until things can smooth over. Pray your sisters make exemplary matches and in due time all can be well again.

Your loving mother.

March 20,
Bangor Hall

Dearest Mama,

The mail is incredibly slow. I am beside myself, for Captain Tenby has made no contact and I fear for his health. I am hoping that the moment I send this to you, I shall receive word from him and all my panic will be for nothing. If he does not, it must indicate he is in a terrible situation. Why else would he not to be able to send a message of any kind after such a long time?

It should be a lovely spring day here, but it's raining and miserable. If I cannot return to London, at least let me hasten to Bath, where I shall be with you again and amongst some proper company. There is absolutely nothing to do here. The Marquess and his wife are trying their best to be accommodating, but their newly wedded bliss is making them unsuitable for company. I believe Amelia is involved in reading business letters!

Yes, business letters!

You think I'm a disgrace? The lady of the house is conducting trade. Even the Dowager is involved! Clearly this is not a fit place for me to be in residence. If you are concerned for our family's reputation, you should send for me immediately, so that I am not tainted by association.

I shall make haste to Bath at your first word.

In my heart, I know Captain Tenby is completely honorable. Once he knows where I am, he will come and claim me and we shall be wed. Then all will be well.

Your darling Demeter.

April 10,
        Bangor Hall,

Dearest Mama,

I pray your most recent letter is on its way to me, but I could not wait another day longer. I am ruminating into complete mold. I have more cobwebs than a scarecrow and I am wearing the same clothes day after day! Partly because there are no events to attend, but mostly because I have only one warm dress to keep me comfortable in this inclemency.

Will the rain never stop? There is so little to do here, I have even taken up walking along the Menai. It is a lovely river. The tides are dramatic and distracting – somewhat. There, I have found one good thing to report. That does not, however, cancel out all the many dull things here. I am not ashamed to admit I am so lonely here, I have taken to talking with the Lord's overseer and we discuss crop rotations!

Let me come home, or at the very least, let me come to Bath!

Your darling Demeter.

Ps, The Marchioness and I are friends. She is a rather lovely and jovial person, despite dealing in trade. I was correct, she is still heavily engaged in business. Even worse, I have found the business a rather pleasant distraction. Are you completely mortified by my utter fall from grace? Then send word and I shall be at your side.

April 20,
        Bangor Hall

Dearest Mama,

I can only assume your most recent letter to me was waylaid. The weather here is ghastly. That's not merely my opinion alone. The families here are saying it's unusually cold and wet. I'm sure it's much more pleasant in Bath. Tell me all about Persephone and Hestia's seasons. I cannot obtain any information about London society all the way out here. I have taken to reading the news sheets but they are filled with reports of crops and sale prices, and of course the awful weather. At least I have things to discuss with the overseer.

Please let me come to Bath. Please?

D-

April 25,
    Bangor Hall

Dearest Mama,

I know you have not had a chance to reply, but I miss you so much. I even miss Persephone and Hestia. It rains every day here. I have attached a cutting from the newssheet describing how bad the weather is. It's all anyone can talk about, so it's not just me complaining of the damp.

D-

May 10
Bath

My dutiful daughter,

I have forbidden your mother to write any more missives to you. I have also withheld your last two letters from her sight. Your earlier correspondence has caused her terrible distress. The weather in Bath is just as awful as it is in north Wales. Did you think it was only raining in Bangor? To specifically punish you?

I beg you to be sensible to your situation, and the strain you have placed the entire family into because of your failed elopement, and how it reflects on your Mama and myself as parents of such a willful and disobedient child.

It has now been several months and your captain is nowhere to be found. What will arrive first, Christmastide or your Captain?

At least you are not in London to ruin your sisters' seasons. They have borne up magnificently under the pressure of scandal and catty gossip. Despite their dowries and your aunt and uncle's best efforts, they have yet to find a suitable match. I am now indebted to them.

Speaking of dowries, it pains me to report that Captain Tenby has not made contact to ask for yours; another reason to believe he has no intention to wed you.

You shall remain exactly where you are until you can prove you have developed a sense of responsibility for your damaging actions.

To this point, your new charges will arrive soon.

They are a gift from the Prince Regent. As you claim to be in dire need of distraction, this will do well for you. Look after them and keep them safe and out of trouble. They must be in excellent condition for the Prince's visit. Do not disturb your mother further, she is at her wits' end.

Yours etc.,

CHAPTER 1: MARRIAGE, SHE WROTE

May 29, 1816
Bangor Hall
North Wales

Her father's letter burned worry into Demeter Mellingham's heart as she headed down the stairs to breakfast. She stopped by the tall windows of Bangor Hall to read it again in the watery morning light. There it was, written in her father's own hand – the prince regent would be visiting!

How would they get Bangor Hall ready in time for such an esteemed guest? More importantly, would it stop raining by then?

Even more importantly, when was the prince planning on arriving?

Shaking her head with concern, her attention wandered to the nearby flowing waters of The Menai Strait. This morning the banks were high. Water lapped the hedgerow at the bottom garden. The green lawn had developed brown patches as the grass drowned in the wet, salty water. The foreman was out there, checking the water levels or whatever it was he did for the Rosstrevors. From the grin on his face, his chance of ending up even more drenched than usual seemed to delight him.

At that moment, he turned and saw Demeter standing on her dry side of the glass. A flinch of discovery caught her and she had to pretend she was looking at the river, not he. The man touched his cap in greeting and sent her a smile that cut through the gloom.

The rogue.

It wasn't Demeter's fault the foreman reminded her of Captain Tenby. He had curly dark hair that was often wet from the rain, and a strong brow with slightly wild eyebrows. From this distance, she wondered if his eyes were the same light brown as her gallant captain's.

Toasted bread aromas wafted up the stairs. Time to get to the breakfast room. The bright yellow curtains in here fought a losing battle with the grey skies on the other side of the window panes. Demeter made a swift curtsey to all and proceeded to fill her plate with toast and butter, then she checked the table for the dish of marmalade.

Excellent, there was plenty left.

Her mind snagged on some of the words in her father's letter. Two new charges? That concerned her even more than the prince's visit. They would be arriving soon, according to his letter, and they would need to be in … what had her father written? 'excellent condition' for the visit. What an odd way to speak about people.

Poor lambs, being sent away from the palace! What apparently dreadful thing had they done to irritate the prince?

Lack of sunlight was making so many people melancholy. Perhaps there was not much sun in London either? Father has said the weather was just as bad in Bath, so it was possible the capital could be shrouded in wet as well. Maybe that was why Prince George was sending people away – he was in bad humors from the poor weather.

Whoever they were, they would need to get used to the early mornings here. Demeter was doing her best, but she was always last to arrive for breakfast. These days, she arrived early enough to greet the Rosstrevors before they went about their duties. She was glad to have arisen early this morning, because she needed to speak with them.

As she took her seat, Demeter knew the entire household would be whirling faster than 'The Swellies' which appeared without warning in the Menai waters, once she shared the news.

She put her bundle of letters down and retrieved the most recent epistle to make sure she was reading it correctly.

"Salutations of the morning, my lord, my lady. I don't mean to throw the house into disarray, but my father sends word that the prince regent will be visiting."

Time stood still. The Marquess froze in place, a fork of food half-way to his mouth. His mother's mouth fell open, then she closed it with a snap. His wife's brows rose high and stayed there.

Eventually, David Rosstrevor put his fork down and spoke. "The Prince Regent? Is coming here?"

"That's what it says in my father's letter," Demeter confirmed, folding the paper to the pertinent part, and passing it to him so that he may read it for himself.

He immediately handed it to Lady Rosstrevor, who said something like, "Does it, now?"

The Dowager rose from her seat and moved to her ladyships' shoulder, her mouth turning down at the edges as she also read the words.

Amelia Rosstrevor read the letter out loud, "New charges arrive soon ... They must be in excellent condition for the Prince's visit." Oh goodness, there it is. Then he goes on to say, "Do not disturb your mother further, she is -"

"- That part isn't important." Demeter interrupted, hoping to retrieve the paper and spare any comments about the rest of its contents. Then the Rosstrevors would truly know how disappointed the Mellinghams were about what she'd done. They knew to some extent, of course, as her father had written and asked them to take her in, all those months ago.

Amelia Rosstrevor's brows dropped into a crease. She nodded her head as she counted the weeks dates in her head. "We don't know when, but I do hope it does not occur during my confinement."

The dowager spoke. "It is an honor to receive such a visit, but it would have been prudent to check with us first." She turned to her son and said, "Are you sure the prince did not write you?"

David Rosstrevor paled somewhat and cleared his throat. "I have seen no such correspondence. Are we sure the prince means to visit us *here*? Perhaps your father means he'll be in the general vicinity. How odd that he should know before we do?"

"I will write my father for further details," Demeter said. "I agree, it's difficult to ascertain. My first thought was that the Prince was coming here, to Bangor Hall. Also, my father says the prince is sending me two charges to take care of. Why are people referred to as 'charges' instead of 'people', and why would he not check with your good selves before sending more guests here? Has he sent an earlier letter directly to you asking about this?"

Lady Rosstrevor turned to her husband and said, "We've had nothing directly from your father since you arrived. We did find one yesterday, which was for you. It must be the one you are showing us now. We did write to him at the time of your arrival to let him know you were safe and well. He replied with a brief note to say that he was satisfied with the news. Then we heard nothing." The lady absently rubbed her palm over her belly. "This is the first correspondence we've seen from him since then. I am relieved you saw fit to show it to us, but also, I am discombobulated as to its contents."

The Dowager Marchioness shook her head and made her way back to her seat. "It's most vexing. Until now I would not have thought the prince cared much about us. He's not trying to reclaim Caernarfonshire is he?" She refilled her teacup and asked nobody in particular, "Perhaps he is planning a procession of some kind? The cathedral is lovely. I'm looking forward to seeing my grandchild baptized there. I shall write to Dean Warren and ask if he has any information."

David Rosstrevor shook his head and turned to Demeter. "It's as well that you brought this to our attention. Please write to your father for more information about when the prince will arrive and what his needs may be. While you're at it, ask him for the name of a secretary or courtier who is organizing the visit. It's a strange thing that we should be hearing about this most important news via your father, and not from someone within the palace itself."

Demeter read the letter again and could not for the life of her work out what her father meant. Why would the Prince of Wales be visiting such an out-of-the way place?

If only her mother had been the author of the letter! The very first line would have focused on the Prince's visit. The rest of the letter would have been dense with detail, not added as an afterthought at the end of a thorough dressing-down about her failure to wed.

Click here to keep reading *Marriage, She Wrote.*

ALSO BY EBONY OATEN

New Series - Runaway Christmas Brides

My True Love Fled With Me

Available August 26, 2026

Unsuitable Suitors (Sweet Regency)

1. The Christmas Marquess
2. Miss Remington's Steely (Christmas) Resolve
3. Marriage, She Wrote
4. All Roads Lead To Earls
5. Fetch The Christmas Earl
6. A Swain For Miss Penhurst
7. Her Christmas Temptation

Regency Romps (Sexy Regency)

1. There's Something About Miss Mary
2. Hot August Night
3. Scandalous Charlotte
4. Weekend At Baron E's
5. Duke Around and Find Out
6. Romancing The Stone-Cold Rogue
7. Risqué Business
8. Bad News Bonklesford
9. Coming Up In The World

www.ebonyoaten.com

THE BOOKSHOP BELLES

NOVELS CO-WRITTEN
WITH CATHERINE BILSON:

Estelle's Ardent Admirer

Marie's Merry Gentleman

Louise's Christmas Champion

Bernadette's Dashing Doctor

THE BOOKSHOP BELLES

In the bustling market town of Hatfield, the four Baxter sisters are doing their best to manage Baxter's Fine Books while their father is away on a book-buying expedition in France. Each sister has her own strengths and dreams, but keeping the bookshop afloat will require all their combined wit, determination, and courage.

From fiery debates to slow-burn romance, the sisters find themselves tangled in unexpected love stories that challenge their beliefs and test their hearts.

• **Estelle**, the practical eldest, clashes with a charming gentleman who upends her carefully ordered life.

• **Marie**, the steady and sensible sister, is stranded in a snowbound castle with a brooding earl and his mischievous sons.

• **Louise**, the no-nonsense protector of the family, finds herself drawn to a towering former soldier with secrets of his own.

• **Bernadette**, the compassionate healer, must learn to work with a dashing doctor whose modern methods challenge everything she holds dear.

Set against the backdrop of a cosy bookshop and a charming Regency town, *The Bookshop Belles* is a heartwarming series about love, family, and the courage it takes to follow your heart.

Perfect for fans of sweet historical romance, these witty, slow-burn love stories feature strong heroines, dashing heroes, and happy endings without on-page sexual content.

ABOUT EBONY OATEN

Ebony Oaten loves history, but doesn't like living through it.

She is especially glad she was not around during the Regency era, as she would most likely have died in infancy from asthma, or something hideous like diphtheria. In the unlikely event that she'd made it to adulthood, she would have probably been a scullery maid or a lowly servant, as she 'talked too much and didn't pay attention' because ADHD diagnoses hadn't been invented.

Grab a free, sweet Regency romance novella and join her reading community here.

Or, if you like spicier reads, grab a free, steamy Regency romance novella and join her reading community here.

(You can grab both, and she'll delete email double-ups, it's all good.)

You'll find her website, full of Regency romance catnip, at www.ebonyoaten.com

facebook.com/EbonyOaten
threads.com/@ebony_mckenna